Concrete People and the Ring of Empathy

Eric Schatz

iUniverse, Inc.
Bloomington

Concrete People and the Ring of Empathy

This is a work of fiction. All of the characters, names, incidents, organizations, and dialogue in this novel are either the products of the author's imagination or are used fictitiously.

iUniverse books may be ordered through booksellers or by contacting:

iUniverse
1663 Liberty Drive
Bloomington, IN 47403
www.iuniverse.com
1-800-Authors (1-800-288-4677)

Because of the dynamic nature of the Internet, any web addresses or links contained in this book may have changed since publication and may no longer be valid. The views expressed in this work are solely those of the author and do not necessarily reflect the views of the publisher, and the publisher hereby disclaims any responsibility for them.

Any people depicted in stock imagery provided by Thinkstock are models, and such images are being used for illustrative purposes only.

Certain stock imagery © Thinkstock.

ISBN: 978-1-4502-9492-8 (sc)
ISBN: 978-1-4502-9491-1 (dj)
ISBN: 978-1-4502-9493-5 (ebk)

Library of Congress Control Number: 2011901689

Printed in the United States of America

iUniverse rev. date: 3/11/2011

*To the shelter-less, the survivors,
the men and women who struggle to make their voices heard.
May this book unlock your muted cries
and open the hearts and minds of the world
to the seeds of homelessness.*

Acknowledgments

Special thanks goes out to the individuals who invited me into their world and shared their experiences with me. You will never be forgotten. Dad and Pam, thank you for your love and support, you've been amazing. To Illuminata, who's heart has helped to guided me through all of the ups and downs, our times is far from up. To my brother Steve, where do I begin? You've come to my rescue time and time again, words cannot express my gratitude for your kindness. To my family in Silver City NM, our circle will never be broken, and the warmth from your love will never be snuffed out. Journey well my friends! And to the amazing team at iUniverse, you know who you are, thank you for your guidance, treasured knowledge and calmness during the hazy times. And to the spirit that moves through all things, much gratitude for the blessings of this life and the potent gift of empathy.

Contents

Introduction

In the winter of 1992, I set out on a journey to understand how a person can fall to great misfortune and wind up on the streets, begging for his livelihood. What I found changed my life.

Within these pages are the stories of individuals I interviewed from 1992 to 1994. Although some of the narrative is fictional, the stories of the people are unaltered, staying true to the raw essence of their accounts.

To know the perils of the less fortunate is to walk in the same ragged shoes they travel in: lacking a haven, with no bed to rest their heads on after a long day of wandering the streets; looking for the support of strangers, begging for enough cash for a sandwich and drink, dimes and quarters clanging in a used Styrofoam cup.

Can you imagine being—or have you ever been—one of the destitute and unwanted; another casualty in a society that looks away, hoping the problem will vanish like a bad dream?

Have you ever slept on a park bench or behind a dumpster, hiding from the cruel winter winds? Have you ever wondered how someone could live in a makeshift cardboard shelter alongside rats and vermin?

I believe to truly understand the experience of the less fortunate, one needs to stand side by side with them and listen to their stories. Imagine leaping into the past lives of others, getting a glimpse of what made them the people they have become.

What a gift to be able to journey through time and space to a stranger's doorstep, viewing the trauma he or she has gone through, and in the process understanding him or her better. Through the power of empathy, our main character is able to view key moments in the lives of a group of homeless people, thus helping him to understand their position in life.

Rick has a curious disposition, always questioning the ways of society, seeking answers in the dark alleyways of life. It isn't until the morning after one of the worst dreams of his life that he feels the push to seek the answer to one of his deepest questions: "Where are the seeds of homelessness sown?"

His journey leads him to the unlikeliest of places, and with the help of a magical ring, he is able to glimpse into the lives of the people he interviews.

In writing this book, I hope to bring forth another viewpoint on the subject of homelessness: to transport the reader back in time, to the origins of individual trauma, where the seeds of addiction and neglect were first planted; and, in the end, to give a more empathetic view of this disturbing problem.

Chapter 1:
Down the Rabbit Hole

To be shelterless and alone in the open country, hearing the wind moan and watching for day through the whole long weary night; to listen to the falling rain, and crouch for warmth beneath the lee of some old bark or rick, or in the hollow of a tree—are dismal things—but not so dismal as the wandering up and down where shelter is, and beds and sleepers are by thousands; a homeless rejected creature.
—Charles Dickens

The wind whipped hard against my cold, numb ear, while splintery wooden slats pressed against my stiff, rigid back. I could hear the flapping of wings swiping against soppy pavement. The light of morning stung my eyes as I scanned the surroundings.

I sat on a park bench in some obscure city park, clothes tattered, skin leathery and coarse. Lightning-shock ripped through my body as my mind awoke to this surreal reality.

"Where am I?" I thought, gripping the cold metal armrest. An empty wine bottle half covered with a ripped paper bag lay in my lap where I had cradled it all night like a lone infant.

"How did this happen?" I wrangled. "I'm not homeless! I'm an art student! I have an apartment on the South Side! This can't be happening ..."

Before my mind had a chance to implode, I heard a faint and distant beeping. Turning to my left, floating two feet away, were a pair of my own eyes looking back at me.

A clone of myself slowly materialized around the eyes, dressed in clean clothes and holding a tape recorder up to my ragged, homeless double. I tried to speak, but the clean-clothed me interrupted by making that same beeping noise, now growing louder.

"Beep … beep!" he said, moving closer, staring blankly into my eyes.

My double held out his hand and spoke in a metallic tone, "See for yourself and you will become wise."

A shiny silver ring appeared in his palm. It had an opened eye on the front, a red gemstone resting in the place of the pupil. Before I knew it, the ring was gone and had reappeared on my right pointer finger. My finger tingled as I tried to pry it loose.

"Get it off!" I implored, sweat dripping from my cheek. The ring seemed to be glued on, and the more I pulled on it, the tighter it squeezed my finger. I could feel the blood collecting, building up pressure, but before it could explode my clone-self distracted me by waving his hands wildly.

"Beep … wake up … beep … wake up to reality!" he said as he waved his hand over my eyes. "Beep … you will now see them … beep … see them!"

His eyes became more intense as I began to shake, sweat collecting in my earlobes.

"Wha-what do you mean wake up? See them … Who're *them?* I …"

The world turned gray and swirled to black, transporting me to another place.

Beep, beep, beep!

The fiery red lights on the alarm clock glared at me, jolting me out of bed. I shook my hand manically, trying to get the demon ring off, but my finger was bare.

The room was quiet, but in my mind, that alarming scene played over and over again. Over the coming days, I became obsessed with this dream. I needed to explore it, to find its deeper meaning.

December was a blur. Sleep came infrequently as I wrestled with my dreams, fearing a return to that dismal park bench.

This is where my journey began: chasing a dream down the rabbit hole, like Alice, racing to catch the greater meaning of life.

On any other Monday at 3:00 p.m., I would be hauling my fifteen-pound book bag across a quarter-mile bridge past two or three destitute people, pondering the severity of the homeless situation in this city and others in the wealthiest country of the world. But with my own homeless nightmare crowding my waking world, I became preoccupied with the intense feelings it was generating. I needed to find real answers to real questions. Like, where does it originate, and how can I *really* understand it?

Have you ever had a fever that clung tightly to your head, refusing to let go, like being swallowed by a hungry boa constrictor? Well, a similar fever overcame me, holding me down, squeezing my lungs tight. The only way to confront this fearfulness and break the spell it had cast on me was to face its source. So a few days and many more nightmares later, I set out with a mini voice recorder and questions swirling in my mind. What I found would change my life forever.

Chapter 2:
Rocky

One of the greatest casualties of the war in Viet Nam is the
Great Society ... shot down on the battlefield.
—Martin Luther King Jr.

My hand cramped up as I slid the rendering marker across the clear tracing paper. I never did like drawing cars, let alone rendering them for a grade. The windshield looked messy and the tires were lopsided. It looked more like a Salvador Dali circus-mobile than a sports car. Scanning the room, I could see all the other more-detailed drawings of sportsters, and I felt utterly embarrassed about mine.

The hands on the classroom clock seemed to move slower and slower. My attention turned to the large window facing the city skyline. I moved my chair toward the window to get a better view of the street twenty stories below. My eyes fixed upon a man sitting on the curb, yelling at passersby. His head jerked and his arms mimed some battle scene from a war movie.

Who was this man? Where did he come from? Just then, I remembered I had brought my mini tape recorder with me.

"This may be my opportunity!" I said, packing up my book bag and heading out of the classroom.

Lunchtime in the city. People rush from work to café, hoping to combine food consumption with relaxation. I never understood how anyone could relax with so much adrenaline pumping all around them. But when time is money, digesting food is the last thing on anyone's mind.

Lunchtime for the homeless can never really be planned; it comes whenever food is available. They are opportunists, like animals in the wild, such as the coyote, who, when food is scarce, will eat scraps from humans or a carcass of an old kill. In a survival situation, when the opportunity is right, a person without the luxury of money will take whatever he is given.

I strolled down the sidewalk, seeking the man I had seen a few moments ago. I came to a dead stop, as if some invisible force blocked me from moving forward. Panic filled my mind as I stood helpless, unable to move. I looked down at the ground in bewilderment. Something shiny caught my attention: a silver ring lying at the base of a newspaper stand.

The ring sparkled in the high-noon sun like a polished precious stone. Its silvery glow seemed to release the spell I was under and I was able to move freely. I knelt down to pick it up. It felt almost electric as I grasped it and wiped off the grime from the streets. A ruby gemstone sat snug in the front of the ring, just like the one I had seen in my dream.

My heart knew what needed to happen next.

I held the ring a quarter of an inch away from my finger, and it slid on as if it were magnetized to my flesh. Energy jolted through my body, and the ring glistened. I stood there for a few minutes, admiring my new treasure, sliding it on and off, making sure it wasn't a permanent fixture like in the dream. A few moments later I remembered my task. I spotted the man I was hunting for. He disappeared down an alleyway, so I headed in that direction.

When I turned the corner, he stood before me, face swollen like a bruised, overripe peach, crusted with day-old blood. As he raised the torn bag containing a bottle of Mad Dog 20-20 to his lips, I noticed that only two fingers remained on his left hand.

This man was indeed like a wild coyote, his eyes squinting under a low brow, nose sniffing the frosted air. I approached him with caution and explained what I was doing.

He stared me down for a few seconds, scanning my body as if trying to detect any bullshit or weapons, then nodded his head. He squinted at me like a tired old mangy dog, then spoke.

"I'm Rocky. You see them fingers? You see this face? It ain't from no beauty school! This here's from the skids."

His raspy, booming voice made my insides jump.

"I been out here for over twenty years and the streets ain't been nice!"

He slouched to pick up a half-used cigarette butt, straightened it with his two shaky fingers, struck a match on the side of the building, took a drag, and continued.

"The government put me here. I fought five years in the jungles across the ocean. Never could understand why."

His taut, leathered skin seemed to prevent him from showing any expression. Listening to his story, I began to feel dizzy. The ring on my finger was glowing. The man's face started to blur and the city slowly vanished.

I reached out to grab at anything to anchor me, but some unseen force caught me and hurled me through the crisp air. I hugged my trembling body as I tumbled through the swirling darkness.

Upon opening my eyes, I found myself high above a jungle canopy. The ring's ruby glowed bright, illuminating the lush green web of plant life like a floodlight. Flashes of light and the boom of gun fire broke the silence of this once serene place. Shadowy outlines moved about, as if floating over the vine-covered jungle floor. They whispered in some foreign tongue.

The dizziness hit me again, and before I had a chance to survey the foreign landscape, I was surrounded by gunfire. The spirit shadows had transformed into soldiers, some American and some Vietnamese. Lightning blasts blanketed the green denseness, while human flesh and limbs were propelled through the air. People were dying all around me and I felt helpless from where I observed.

A familiar voice called out to a fellow soldier.

"Don't you worry, Bud. I got ya!"

A man quickly yet gently scooped up another man in his arms. As they ran toward me I remained frozen, elevated one foot from the ground. I held my arms outstretched, as if to block them from running into me. Just before we collided, I felt as if I was consumed by fireworks. When the sparks faded, the jungle began to move. My legs felt tremendous strain and pressure as I sprinted through the thick foliage. What happened next stunned me to my core.

I stopped to rest at a nearby stream, and as I slowly lowered my head to look to the ground, I saw that *I* was carrying the fallen soldier. My hand, sticky and wet with blood, held the man's intestines in his abdomen so they would not spill onto the jungle floor.

Panic hit me like a Mac truck as I realized that I had somehow become this hero soldier! The man in my arms mumbled something incoherent as I looked into his wide, terrified eyes.

I lowered my head to hear him better, and his faint voice became clearer. He said, "I … I ain't gonna make it, Rocky! I'm re … real cold, Rocko …"

Without thinking, I said in a rough whisper, "You're gonna be just fine, kid! We're getting closer to the rendezvous point!"

This was the moment I realized I was living a piece of Rocky's past—the man I was interviewing. He was a true hero, and I had the honor of witnessing a moment of his heroism. A sudden wave of emotion overcame me, and the dizziness returned. My head pounded and my hair stood electric; my ring finger throbbed as the red glow pulsed. The jungle began to move. All of the blasts and blood swirled into one as I felt myself being pulled back to my own world. I felt nauseous as my body somersaulted through time, swallowed in darkness.

The cold bite of winter and the smell of car exhaust filled the air. A light nudge on my shoulder brought my attention to the present.

"Hey, you still with me boy?"

I shook my head, rubbed my tearing eyes, apologized, and he continued.

"I get drunk and go a little crazy as you can see on my face," Rocky said, framing the left side of his face with his thumb and index finger. "This happened last night. Some thugs beat me to a pulp. The swelling will go down and the cuts will heal, but my trust in humanity won't. Check this out," he said boastfully, pointing to his covered left hand. "I lost three fingers to the streets. This one I lost to frostbite, this one I did myself, and this one someone else took."

He held up his hand, half covered by his ripped coat sleeve. The sight of his hand, like a diseased tree branch, produced the same response I had experienced moments ago. My head began to spin again and the city evaporated into pools of gray, while the ring repeated that same trance-inducing glow. Confusion overtook me as I looked down a dark, damp alleyway. The sound of overturned trashcans and screams filled the night air.

Trash-filled wind funnels whipped around packed dumpsters, while alley cats scrambled to hide in dark corners. Two men were slouched over water pipes, moaning. It seemed as though I had arrived in the middle of a battle.

Two large shadows loomed over a curled-up figure. The larger of the two men spoke in a deep, guttural tone.

"Now why did ya gotta go and do that? You just had to go and break some bones, now, didn't ya? You know da rules, Rocky. You ain't got no money to give, then we gotta take somethin' from you!"

Next, I heard a wet snap, like a branch being pruned, followed by a blood-curdling shriek. Rocky threw his head back, head-butting his attacker. The other man swiftly kneed Rocky in the mid-section. The bass thud echoed off of the brick walls, sending chills up my spine.

Once again, I had been transported to Rocky's past. The four men passed me unnoticed, leaving Rocky where he lay in a pool of his own blood. Then they vanished into the busy city night. I rushed anxiously over to Rocky's shaking body, coiled in the fetal position.

Before I could say anything, my body began to shake. My arms turned iridescent as I collapsed face-first into Rocky. Our bodies merged into one another amid the prowling rats. Pain flamed through my left hand and my face throbbed as I struggled to see through swollen eyes.

Damn! Here I am again, I thought. A feeling of dread overwhelmed me.

"Oh, God! Please get me outta here!" I screamed, cradling my hand against Rocky's stomach. Fire escapes and dark windows blurred into one as I slipped into unconsciousness.

An ambulance siren brought me back. I held my left hand tight against my heart, my eyes wide, while my body trembled. The ring seemed to vibrate. Rocky was still talking, unaware of my crisis.

"The government just throws its people out on the streets like bad eggs. You know, I even got a Purple Heart for my courage!" He pointed to his chest, pride painted on his face. "I left my courage in Nam. Got so much hate and mistrust runnin' through these veins I can't even look at people straight no more. Only reason I can do it with you is 'cuz I had my shot of Mad Dog."

His words intoxicated me. I felt his high and dreaded the inevitable crash.

"What people don't understand is that us bottom-feeders are survivors. When the shit hits the fan all you people who depend on all this," his arms wind-milled in circles, "will suffer, and we will thrive. That's right, *we* the scum, *we* the vagrants, *we* the I-want-a-quarter-for-a-cup-of-coffee will be the ones that will inherit this place, 'cuz we know how to survive. We've been through the barbed-wire forest."

My hand ached again and my head throbbed as I felt his pain. By witnessing parts of his life experience, I already had a better understanding of his situation. As he continued, I became more relaxed.

"I ain't got no good things to say. As you can see, I'm a piece of raw meat, a scrap for people to walk on. I bleed only for my own screwed-up life. Got no one else but me to look at in that puddle over there." He pointed to a large pothole filled with water. Oil swirled over the top.

"But hey, don't feel sorry for me. Don't even pay me no mind."

I felt his grief. His heart had been ripped out of his chest again and again, and his cries for help had been muted by those he served to protect in Viet Nam. These were the origins of his hate. I felt his deep yearning for peace, but there was no peace in his chaos-filled mind and heart. I struggled to keep my own heart intact.

A pigeon swooped down from its roost. Rocky watched it with eyes wide as he continued, "If I could fly I would fly far away from here, back to that jungle. In the bush I was doin' somethin' that I was good at. I had a purpose. Maybe that purpose was distorted, but I had some kind of footing. I was grounded."

He stomped his left foot firmly on the ground, bootlaces jumping. "Only purpose I have out here is to keep this heart beatin', as black as it may be."

For a moment, I caught him smile. Maybe it was the unexpected warm breeze that swirled down from above, or maybe it was his pride. Either way, it was a moment of peace.

Then the cold bite of winter returned as Rocky stared blankly at a nearby billboard with big gold letters that said, WIN $1,000,000 INSTANTLY!

"Not much more to say," he continued. "Can't wait to get that next sip."

His bottle lay empty next to him, rocking in the breeze.

"That's the only thing I have to look forward to. Just sittin' on my stoop, watchin' the blur of the world and my life pass by."

An uneasy feeling came over me. I felt genuinely sad for this man. But I felt hopeless too, not knowing what I could do for him or people like him. I am one person and there are so many of them. I envisioned hundreds of homeless people swirling around me. I felt as if I were being flushed down a gigantic commode with nothing to grab onto.

My vision was interrupted by a loud nearby voice.

"Hey man, you got the juice!" Rocky yelled, eyeing another homeless man about fifty feet away.

The other man pulled out a large bottle of wine from his dusty trench coat. Rocky let out a joyful yell and hobbled over to the man. Several others joined in as they passed the bottle around.

A few minutes later the small crowd had dispersed and Rocky limped back to me, stumbling over his bootlaces.

"Ohh, you're still here?" he said as I shifted my weight, balancing myself as he got closer.

"You saw what just happened, right? Well, that's everyday life for me. Just waitin' for that next drink. I'm just gonna end with this, you follow?"

He pointed to my mini tape recorder. I started the tape rolling and he continued.

"So if you see a busted-up old man sittin' on the street corner," he said, pointing to himself, "and you give him a quarter, you can be certain that it's goin' towards a bottle. You ain't killin' me. You just helpin' to ease my pain and get me through the day. Got to go. Someone got some Mad Dog!"

His bent body disappeared into a crowd of business suits and briefcases. I stood frozen to the ground. I had just been catapulted through time and space, in and out of insanity in the blink of an eye. Now, here I stood, eyes wide and mind stunned with the city buzzing and swirling around me. My body needed sleep, but something deep within urged me to move on. I knew that the ring had something to do with viewing Rocky's past, but I was still baffled by the whole experience.

"Maybe one more interview will give me the answers I'm looking for," I said, staring into space.

The night was young and there were many more questions that needed answering. And there, standing straight in front of me, were a whole group of prospects for my next interview.

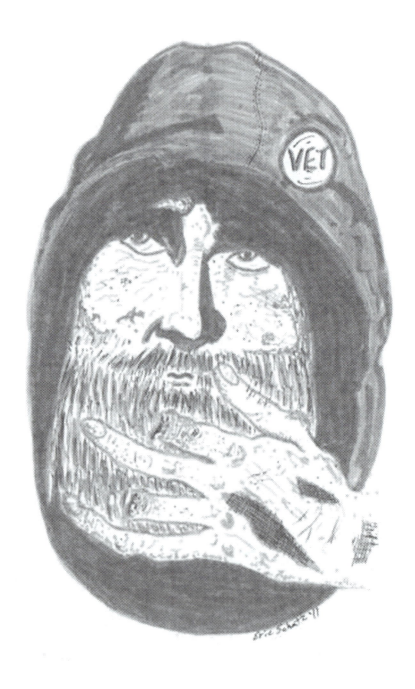

Chapter 3:
Jerry

You take my life when you take the means whereby I live.
—William Shakespeare

My mouth felt dry and parched like the Sahara. I hadn't had a drink in half a day, yet my mind urged me forward. The car garage across the street had a water fountain, so I quenched my thirst and then rushed back over to view the small gathering of homeless people. One of them drew me toward him.

His wire-rimmed glasses sat crooked on his bantam nose, while the midday sun revealed the fine scratches on his right lens. He was a tall, lanky man wearing a tan leisure suit, crotch stained brown, sleeve cuffs worn and frayed. He watched wide eyed as I approached, rocking nervously and moving his lips as if he were lecturing to cold rushing wind.

Nervously, I rubbed the red stone on the ring. *Will I journey into this man's past, like I did with the other guy?* I asked myself.

I breathed deeply, preparing myself for the unknown, and then stepped off the curb. The brisk winter winds seemed to usher me across the street, my legs struggling to keep up the pace. My mind raced as I searched for a way to open a dialogue.

Our eyes met through the steam from an exhaust vent. I nodded, bearing a friendly smile, and he invited me into his space with a hurried nod. I explained that I was on a quest to find out how people become homeless. Immediately his eyes lit up and he began to talk. I fumbled for my voice recorder and pressed the record button.

"I've waited a long time for this—I mean, telling my story and all," he said in a high, mousey voice. "Anyway, my name is Jerry, and a woman brought me to the streets. Back in '72 my wife set me on fire to get my insurance money."

He looked skyward, bottom lip extended, eyes squinting as if to hold back tears.

"I worked in the Belfor Steel for four hard years, sweat to the bone and nearly broke my back. And all it took was a little gas and a match. She was heartless. I lay there, skin melting to the mattress, and she just walked out."

Despite the thirty-degree winds whipping icy needles through my down coat, I began to sweat profusely. That familiar feeling came over me—that dizzy, spinning loss of control. The world around me erupted into flames, red as the stone on my finger, engulfing everything in a blaze of fury. I felt as if my soul had combusted, and the conflagration took over my mind. I drifted away, a spark in the breeze.

I came to, crouched before an unmade bed in a dimly lit room. It felt gray, this room, and I felt something terrible was about to happen. As I stood erect, I scanned the room, finding simple items tossed about. Upon closer inspection of the bed, I discovered the shape of a person beneath the sheet. I detected the faint sound of breathing and then heard the noise of a squeaky door. I turned to see a petite shadow move silently into the room. I knew the figure was a woman by the white nightgown she wore, as well as the curlers wrapped tightly in her hair. I was then horrified to see that in her right hand, she carried a red gas can.

I knew what was going to happen next, and my fear-stricken mind struggled to keep my body grounded to the wood floor. Without warning, I was removed from my position and lodged unclothed under a thin sheet.

Cold splashes cloaked my back, while a strong wafting odor filled my nostrils and stung my eyes. I heard Jerry's voice echo through my mind: "My wife set me on fire ... My wife set me on fire." I felt sickened as I realized what was about to take place.

Just as I threw the sheet back and turned to the perpetrator, I saw a glister of light followed by a streaming flame. The flame cast light over the pyromaniac's face, revealing the most sinister expression. Her possessed face, garnished with a demonic smile, let out the most wicked cackle to ever assault my ears.

The words out of my mouth sounded foreign as I listened with horror.

"No, Darleen! What do you think you're doing?"

The arms I occupied reached out as if to prevent the blaze from spreading further. The flames engulfed the bed and me with a relentless rage upon my body.

Jerry's limbs thrashed in anguish, while through the licks of the fire I saw the demon bride rush out of the room. I could feel the skin on Jerry's legs melt into the mattress. His moans filled my throat while my mind drowned in deliberations of how to escape from this bed of hell.

Just then, without thinking, I tumbled to the floor and grabbed onto the edge of a throw rug. Jerry rolled violently across the floor, extinguishing his body of flames.

My crystalline body floated toward the ceiling as I watched Jerry's quivering figure beneath the thick rug. I witnessed the fire truck arrive with lights gleaming. Flames clawed at the windows as the firemen scrambled up the steps. I wanted badly to see what happened next, but Jerry's voice brought me back.

"Hey, you cold 'er somethin'?" he said with concern as my teeth chattered. I assured him that I had just felt a chill, but I was okay, so he continued to talk.

"So, now I live with another woman called alcoholism. I can't stop! I'm a raving alcoholic!"

His hands trembled as he gazed down at a vacant bottle pitching back and forth in the chilly breeze.

"Now," he continued, "you can talk to the man to my right, Rocky, but he's done. Or you can try talkin' to Tony, the man on my left, but he's gone."

Both men were passed out. Rocky was curled up on an exhaust vent, while the other man, Tony, sat back against the wall with his eyes closed.

"So that leaves me, the man in the middle. If you want a dose of the blues, then I'm your man. I'm still trying to pull myself back to reality."

He tugged on an invisible rope leading to the sidewalk.

"I have a stamp in my coat pocket—that's for the IRS—and in the other pocket a bottle of grapes that calls to me day in and day out."

In that moment, gravity seemed to reverse itself and my gut twisted into a knot. My feet left the ground as I observed Jerry talking to an almost-invisible shell of my grounded self. I floated past windows, viewing men and women in their offices talking on phones, unaware of me drifting by. I looked down to see all the tiny cars and people begin to vanish as I disappeared into a swirl of gray mist. Then I was swallowed in darkness, followed by piercing flashes of light.

I opened my eyes to discover that I had been transported to a stark white room. The floor and walls were covered in puffy white fabric. In front of me was a metal door with a single barred window. The body I occupied felt constricted. I was unable to move anything above my waist; my legs were free, except for an ankle shackle attached to a wall mount.

I was in Jerry's body, in an asylum, wearing a straightjacket. At this point in my journey, I had learned to be still wherever I found myself. Resistance only made things worse.

Faint footsteps sounded in the corridor outside the cell. The footfalls drew near and then stopped just outside the door. A jangling of keys just outside the padded room, and without sanction Jerry's body trembled and dripped with sweat. I began to feel an overwhelming sense of rage take over. No matter how hard I tried, I could not hold those intense feelings back.

The metal door sounded just like I thought it would, its squeaky rusted hinges sending shivers straight through me. A towering man entered the room carrying a stainless steel tray. In a deep, forceful voice, he ordered, "Hey, Jerry! The time has come yet again, my man! Let's go. Ya gotta take yer meds!"

Jerry's head lifted. His eyes met with the large man's orbs, and a feeling of madness overtook me.

"Don't give me that look, Jer! You—"

Jerry spat into his eye. In a flash, the man back-handed Jerry's face, sending his body hurling across the room. Before I could make sense of what was going on, three more men leapt upon Jerry's undulating body, and my lungs began to feel crushed. The weightiness of their bodies was suffocating and I began to panic.

I tried to calm myself, but felt that they really wanted Jerry to suffer. I experienced a sharp stab in my left buttock, and shortly after, a dull heaviness came over Jerry's sweat-drenched body.

The three men left the room but one of them returned, kneeling down beside Jerry and whispered, "Oh yeah, I forgot to give ya this."

He stuck his large index finger down Jerry's throat. I was forced to swallow a large, round object. The man's finger tasted like salty dirt, his skin was dry and rough, and his fingernail had a jagged edge, scraping the inside of Jerry's throat.

The room began to fade, turning to speckles of gray and white. My pulse slowed as I realized that my time in chapter two of Jerry's madness was over. Jerry's voice gradually brought me back, feet planted to concrete, my ears tuned into his words.

"So, I'm on the streets right now. Not too many people have walked in shoes made of this kind of misery. They have no idea what it's like."

As he spoke, I thought to myself, *I, on the other hand, am beginning to get a much clearer picture.*

He continued, "I pissed myself today. I got drunk today. I hurt today. And tomorrow I'll wake up and I'll just hurt again. I've just had to let go of everything. I'm not goin' back in! You know where *back* in is?" he said, his eyes pleading. "South Side detox is where. I can't do it! I just can't go through it again! It felt like an earthquake, end-of-the-world kind, my shakes was so bad."

I felt the quaking he spoke of as my hands began to shake.

"Couldn't even hold a cup of coffee. I just can't bear it no more! The streets got a hold of me somethin' bad. This disease is takin' me in, it's takin' me in! I've been through this detox, through that hospital, been through everything. And the Salvation Army keeps saying, 'Come back, Jerry! Find Jesus!' An' I've beared my cross, and I say, 'Screw Jesus! Screw my Lord 'n Savior!' Fuck 'em all. I'm so tired of bein' sick and tired."

As I stood there, crosses burning in my mind, I felt a deep love for this man. I had witnessed the betrayals of his life, and I understood his situation. As Jerry stood there, tears streaming down his sunken cheeks, without thinking I put my hand on his shoulder. His eyes panned up to mine, and then, with a gleam in his eye, he continued to talk.

"I was a professional cook. I loved cooking for people. It gave me pride. I was an artist too!"

The smile on Jerry's face seemed to part the dark clouds. But as quickly as the sun beamed down upon us, it was gone. Jerry's face turned somber as he watched the gray clouds return.

"And now my art is gone. The kitchen is closed, and I'll never see that stove again. I don't know how long I have out here. It might be six months, might be three. When I scream for help this time, it will be extra loud!" He raised his fist to the heavens. "But I'm scared I won't scream. So just let me freeze to death!"

Jerry's squealing voice drew the attention of some passersby.

"I'll just become part of the sidewalk. You already walk over me anyhow," he said, as if talking directly to the people. "I sleep on a piece of steel. A vent keeps me warm at night. Its warm air keeps me from freezing. Some nights I gotta fight for that vent. It's my life support out here in this frozen city. I just don't know how to stop! I'm out of control!"

I saw how Jerry's life was a nonstop stomach-churning ride that he could not control. I wished I could find that invisible lever to stop his hellish ride and pull him off. But I knew that it was up to him to find that off switch and confront his demons.

As he continued, I felt fatigued and struggled to focus on his story.

"I've earned a lot of sins. Maybe I've taken the sins up myself. Maybe I pissed myself tonight, maybe I … I'll never get rid of these sins. I'm lucky if I can make it to station number one."

He held the cross that hung around his neck, knuckles bleach-white.

"Sometimes I just sit on this curb and wonder why I'm out here! Sometimes I get hungry for a sandwich, and sometimes I just get plain hungry, you know, for life. It hurts, this condition. I hurt inside. It's not my heart—it's my soul! I don't know how to stop this hurt." His voice cracked. "I try to claw it out and I try to shout it out, but I don't want to die, not yet! For now," he continued with a sigh, "I'm just waitin' for the next drink. I need that next drink. I don't know how to get off this drunk!"

He angrily backhanded the brick wall behind him, then examined his hand for any damage.

"All the help in the world won't get me off this drunk. My hand is out, and I wait … I wait for Him—that miracle beyond this concrete, that miracle beyond those skyscrapers. And I wait for the drink to dry … and my heart to heal."

He thanked me for listening to his story, hugged me gently, and then crouched down, staring blankly through the passing traffic. I offered him a dollar but Jerry just stared blankly at me, through me; our time was up.

Chapter 4:
Greg C.

Poverty and homelessness are weapons of mass destruction.
—Dennis Kucinich

I fell asleep in the living room recliner, waking occasionally with thoughts of the day. Outside my second story window, a flurry of snow shrouded the street lights. I couldn't help but wonder where Jerry and Rocky were sleeping. How resilient they must be to survive in such weather.

It was Saturday, and I had nothing planned—just an unfinished school project that could wait until Sunday. Excitement pumped through my veins and my temples throbbed at the prospect of doing another interview. I packed a breakfast, along with my voice recorder, and headed out for another adventure in the lives of others.

My frosted watch read 9:00 a.m. as I crossed the quarter-mile bridge into the city. The breakfast line at the soup kitchen meandered for two blocks like a snow-covered snake awaiting its next meal. A man crouched on a cinderblock away from the crowd. He had gotten his meal and found a spot to eat under the ledge of a fire escape.

His wide-brimmed hat hid his eyes, but his chin could be seen rolling from side to side as he munched his breakfast. I asked if I could join him, and with a gesture of his right hand he patted the snow-outlined spot next to him.

"Go ahead," he said.

His onyx-colored skin blended into the shadow of his hat. I took out my bagel-and-egg sandwich and joined him in eating.

"You ain't from around here, is you?" he said suspiciously.

"No," I said. "Just expanding my horizons."

He cocked his head sideways and looked at me with bewilderment.

"Expanding your ho-ri-zons?" he said, sounding out each letter, then snickering to himself. "Oh well, to each his own," he continued. "My name is Greg C."

He wiped the crumbs off his hand and extended it toward me. I introduced myself, and we shook hands.

"What? You want to interview me or somethin'?"

This caught me off guard. How did he know that?

"It's just that a guy like you—you know, someone that don't fit into a soup line, who says he's 'expandin' his horizons'—usually wants somethin'."

I explained why I was there and he agreed to do the interview, as long as I bought him a cup of coffee. Soon afterward, we sat in a warm café, me with my mint tea and him with his black coffee with extra cream. He said it complemented his skin tone.

We sat in silence for a moment, listening to the soft jazz that drifted through the smoky air. He drew in a deep breath, scanned the room slowly, and began to speak.

"I've been on the streets since I was twelve years old, and that was almost thirty years ago. My pops left me when I was eight."

He looked at me to make sure I was paying attention.

"My mother was feeding me and my younger brother by turning tricks at night. Man, she'd leave us alone the whole night! I'm lucky to be sittin' here."

He gazed into the swirling cream of his coffee with a wistful expression on his face.

"When I was ten years old, a woman and two men came by the house and snatched me and my brother up. Just like that, we was separated! Only thing I could figure was my moms got in some kinda tangle with one of the johns she brought home. Sometimes they be so loaded on blow that they'd tie me up and do unspeakable things to me. My moms just lay there, passed out, gone to the world."

My hand gripped the ceramic mug. The tea within began to ripple from the tremors I started to feel. I was getting used to the devices of the ring. His words became muffled as the café walls collapsed in on each other and my body lifted out of my wooden chair. This time I relaxed into the vertigo and surrendered to the inevitable ride that awaited me. The sound of crying gradually filled my ears, faint at first, then growing, until a baby's shrill cries slashed through my mind.

As I opened my eyes, the blurred image of an infant, fiercely upset, slowly came into focus. My pulse raced as I realized my situation. I looked down toward my hands and noticed that they were light brown in color and much smaller than my own.

The light in the foreign room pierced my sensitive eyes as I acclimated myself to this new place. All images were shadows, blurred into one another. It looked as if I were watching a shadow puppet show whenever anything would move. Bass beats thundered through the room as a screaming vocalist spat out rhymes.

I made out a large man dancing in front of me. His hips gyrated as he stared blankly into my eyes. His gaze felt empty, and at the same time wicked. I began to tremble, frantically looking around at the stained walls and ripped furniture. I noticed a young woman lying sprawled out, legs spread, on a tattered sofa. The youthful woman's thighs were bruised purple and green, her vaginal region splattered with blood and semen. Was this Greg's mom? My mind struggled to believe what I already knew. I was terrified at what might have happened in this place. As her still body began to convulse, I started to cry uncontrollably, but my howls were muffled by a large, sweaty hand.

The towering man's hand covered my whole face. I couldn't breathe under it.

"Y'all best chill yaself lil' man, unless you lookin' ta get cracked!" the large man whispered, tightening his grip over my perspiring face.

Greg whimpered as the man removed his hand. The man's large eyes turned to slits as he squinted, face blazing into fire.

"What'd you say da me?" he said as he raised his right hand, towering inferno, to my little body.

As soon as the man's hand struck, I felt Greg's jaw unhinge. Stars and sparks flew through his mind, while shockwaves passed through his nose, followed by a rush of blood. Before my mind went blank, I remember thinking, *How could anyone destroy a child like that?*

As my body lifted high above the chaos and abuse, I tried to turn my eyes from what was going on, but they were fixed upon Greg's beaten little body. Darkness spared me the rest of the story as I swiftly exited the room.

My tea was slightly cooler than when I had departed, although I had been gone only a few minutes. Greg sipped on his coffee as he continued to talk.

"I was then thrown into the system," he said, gazing at the city traffic. "In one year I went through three foster homes, not to mention being separated from my little brother. Haven't seen him since."

As he talked, I could not imagine being separated from my brother, not to mention my mother.

"One family that I stayed with had too big a heart and couldn't handle all my baggage, while the other two were very abusive. I mean, anything I did, they'd whoop me for. So I decided to hit the skids."

My jaw began to pound and my face felt round and swollen. I wondered if some of those foster families had abused Greg like the man in my vision had. A deep sense of sorrow came over me.

"I ain't got no education, got nothin'! I just go job to job. But if you ain't got no education, you ain't got nothin'. And if you ain't got a high-school diploma, you lost. If you can't read, you can't fill out no application and then you ain't got no job."

He shook his head and paused for a moment. "So, when all this came down hard on my back, I started to get that itch."

We emerged from the café, and Greg talked while snowflakes spiraled down.

"And that itch was only satisfied when I started to steal. And then I got caught, so now I got a police record. And so the hole just kept gettin' bigger, until my ass was sittin' on concrete beggin' for money."

The earth beneath me began to vibrate as I watched my feet sink into the fragmented concrete. The once-hard and jagged cement turned soft and gravy-like as I sank beneath the sidewalk. Greg talked as if the snowflakes were his only audience while I descended. I was encased in the earth below, hearing the hollow footsteps of pedestrians and the murmur of the rushing traffic above.

I melted through a drainage pipe as I descended. When the pipe reached my pituitary gland, my mind fluttered, like the starting of a film projector, the flickering blurs of colored light passing over my vision.

The image of a young adult Greg came into view. He sat at a school desk staring at a word-jumbled chalkboard. No other students were there, and I had the impression he felt ungainly. Greg took out a pocketknife and sank its short pointed blade into the hard wood tabletop. As he etched, his attention became more centered. To see what Greg was doing, I accessed some force deep within me to pull his desk toward me. The room stretched as he approached. Greg now sat below my floating body, still etching into the desk, whispering as he carved. With slurred, frustrated words, he muttered, "I can't stand this no more. I just can't do it!"

I looked to see what he had carved. The letters were jagged and twisted. Graffiti-like, they spelled out, DOOMED.

In that moment, I felt a lifetime of distress and frustration. His mind had been blocked by childhood traumas, and his self-esteem had been extinguished by words of hate. Just as I began to feel his pain, the blurred and choppy film reel flapped and my mind turned screen-white.

Another reel started up, and the screen flickered with more images. A man with a robust afro and meaty sideburns stood by a vintage 1970s Cadillac. I knew this man was Greg as I watched him press up against the driver's door, moving his arms in a swift upward motion.

In mid-flight, I felt the wind caress my hair, and then I was slammed into Greg's body. I felt his rush of adrenaline as he began to breathe arduously. The car door lock began to move and then slowly lift as Greg lifted the door handle.

My heart skipped a beat as Greg slipped behind the driver's seat. He hammered the butt end of a large screwdriver against the steering wheel housing. The casing cracked and fell to the floor, revealing twisted wires. His fingers shook as he rubbed two of the wires together. The engine drowsily began to turn.

"Come on, come on!" Greg coaxed, sweat dripping from under his sideburns. As the car rumbled to a start, the piercing sound of a siren and bright lights struck horror into my mind.

Greg threw his arms on the dash, fists clenched, bathed in the lights of contempt. As he emerged from the Cadi, I exited his shaking body, relieved that this chapter was over.

The rusted pipe that brought me the images of this period in Greg's life had cleared, and I was pulled above ground. I shuddered and drew in a deep breath as I focused on what Greg was saying.

"I've hopped boxcars and trains all across this country. Sometimes you don't even know what town you've ended up in, a stranger in a strange land." He scanned my face. "You can read the faces of people you've never met before. Most of them are saying, 'You don't belong here,' but they are really scared, so they call *the man*. And before you know it you're sittin' behind bars again. I don't want to freeze to death out here. The other night got to zero."

Our cloudy breath swirled in the frosted air as icy chills spread through my body.

"I sleep between two dumpsters. After being out here for so long you ain't no human no more. It's the streets—they take your soul away 'til you be wearin' fur and nails sharp as claws. I have become an animal out here."

His upper lip curled as he stared down the street, past warmly bundled people rushing into the warmth of boutiques and office buildings. He thanked me, then turned to me and said with a smile, "It's survival of the fittest and I'm glad to be alive." He disappeared into a bustle of people.

As I stood there, head tilted back, eyes squinting at fluffy snowflakes, I absorbed all of Greg's story and felt deep respect for him. He was a survivor. He had survived an abusive childhood, incarceration, and now, for nearly thirty years, the cold and ironbound streets.

I thought of the many people I hadn't spoken to yet and felt compelled to move on. Lunchtime had arrived, so I decided to take a break and pick up a sandwich at a nearby deli. I didn't get far before I met my next interview, so I changed my tape and prepared myself for another ride.

Chapter 5:
Carl

Believe, when you are most unhappy, that there is something for you to do in the world. So long as you can sweeten another's pain, life is not in vain.
—Helen Keller

The Salvation Army bell reverberated down the bustling streets, snaking around crowds of holiday shoppers and panhandlers, their arms outstretched, holding paper cups. It looked to me as though more money was falling into the red metal bucket than into the paper cups. The fear that emanated from the shoppers invaded my mind, filling me with anger.

Why are people so intimidated by the tragedies of others? my mind screamed as I remembered the horrors I had just witnessed. I stood on the sidewalk deeply perplexed as I watched the hurried scene around me. I needed reassurance, something to give me some kind of hope for humanity.

I decided to walk off my angst. Maybe the soft whiteness that fell from the sky would nurture my confused mind. As I walked, I heard the faint sound of laughter and singing. As my hidden navigator pulled me toward the source of this joy, the singing became louder. I began to rush, my boots slipping through the slushy gray walkway. As I finally rounded a bend and looked over the heads of a swarm of pedestrians, I saw the face of a singing angel. He stood hugging another man. They laughed and slapped sides while they sang.

"Gonna lay down my sword and shield, down by the river side, down by the river side!" They sang as if no one else were around.

As I approached the men, they finished singing, hugged, and parted ways. I moved closer to the man and noticed that he had only one arm and one leg, propped up by a single crutch. He held a tin cup in his right hand, shaking it as he whistled a soft tune. I had to interview him, but for some reason I was nervous about doing so. It felt as if I were approaching a saint, or a sage of a man. As I stared wide eyed, the man glanced in my direction; our eyes met, and my heart seemed to flutter out of its boney cage. Then he smiled at me, with a warmth that melted my fears.

He nodded his head, signaling me to join him. As I walked over to the whistling man, the sea of people that divided us seemed to part, like liquid flesh and fabric. He placed his cup in a makeshift holder attached to his crutch.

"Hello there," he said as I slid across the icy pavement. I coasted toward him, boots crisscrossing through slush, and came to a halt with both hands on his shoulders. We looked into each other's faces and, without embarrassment, howled with heartfelt joy.

I was stunned. Here I stood, with a stranger, gut convulsing with laughter. I felt at home with him, comfort filling my heart.

"You almost had a spill, didn't ya?" he said, voice shaking with a final chuckle. I nervously apologized, but he assured me that it was his duty to lend a hand.

"You look like a man widalota questions on your mind," he said as I lowered my hands to my sides. I described my project to him and his wide smile grew, covering his whole face.

"Man, you want to interview *me*!" he said, lowering his head as if he had just been struck with heavy shyness.

He went on, "Well, okay then. Mamma always did say, 'You gotta reach out for new experiences.' Okay, here goes somethin'!"

He cleared his throat and continued, "My name is Carl, and as you can see, I'm handicapped. I lost an arm and one leg when I was in the army stationed in Iraq." He pointed east with his nose and then went on.

"It was shrapnel from a landmine. I just remember waking up in the trauma unit with all of these white coats 'n masks hovering over me. I thought, 'Well, I still got one good arm, one good leg. My heart's still beating, and my soul's still intact. I'll live.'"

He shook the right side of his body, as if he were dancing to an invisible song.

"The smile you see on this face comes from God. It don't come from me." He nodded his head heavenward, as if to acknowledge his creator. "You see, the pain in my heart was so big that I could never smile, until one day the warmest feeling came over me. I got up out of bed and smiled. Been smilin' ever since!"

Carl looked at me with joy-filled eyes. I bathed in the delight he felt for life. I was awestruck by the positive outlook Carl had for his situation. He had been through a horrifying event and moved forward with such grace and humility.

I felt high. His blissfulness lifted my feet from my boot prints in the slushy snow. My body elevated above the packed walkway, and I ascended toward a luminescent orb.

I did not want this joy to end. I had finally found someone who had a positive outlook on life, and I felt like I was unable to witness another tragedy. But just as my heart opened, lotus-like, my flesh trembled and my bones began to quake. Concussion blasts heralded me, stinging my ears as I awoke with a mouthful of sand.

Intense sunrays greeted me in this new place. Army fatigues adorned the body I now occupied. The thick fabric protected me from darting debris. Through the rip in my glove, I noticed that my skin had turned chestnut brown. I braced myself, preparing for the intense experience that I knew would come next.

Dirt devils moved across the rocky terrain in slow motion. The scene that unfolded all around was pandemonium, as the brown earth detonated into thousands of pieces. As the ringing in my ears subsided, I made out this bygone sound-scape of piercing blasts.

Trepidation filled me from head to toe as I made my way to the cover of a roadside ditch. I slid down the sand-like soil with more fleetness than expected. As I hit the bottom, I realized that I had rolled on top of a fallen soldier. His eyes stared empty into mine; I was stunned to notice that his ribcage had been split open, entrails covering his lower extremities.

My dry-heaves were interrupted by the cry of another soldier.

"Carl ... help, Carl!" he screamed.

Without thought, I began to claw my way out of the ditch, as if I were piggybacking Carl, feeling his muscles convulse with every movement.

I'm coming. Stay calm, Carl thought as he snaked his way out of the ditch toward the shrapnel-riddled road.

I could feel the sand blasting against Carl's face as he emerged from the grave-like ditch. The thick dust clouds made it hard to see where the distress call had come from, but Carl quickly moved toward the cries with ungainly steps. I could feel his pulse pound beneath taut skin as he approached the fallen comrade. An earth-filled funnel surrounded Carl, keeping him from moving forward. He held his left forearm over his eyes, protecting them from the stinging grains of sand. His boots slammed hard into the earth as he leaned into the fierce wind.

Just then, as Carl started to call out for his comrade, he noticed that his right boot had sunk down into the earth, followed by a vibrating "click." He felt the faint click through his heavy boot, and although the wind made it hard for him to hear, Carl could feel a metallic buzzing noise.

The gusts died just as Carl realized what he had stepped on. He looked down at his left boot and saw what he feared most: a Daisy Cutter, or landmine. He knew that without a bomb specialist, his chances of survival were slim to none.

Looking toward the sky, Carl raised his right arm and shouted, "Give me the strength, Lord!"

He then catapulted his body, twisting in mid-flight as the bomb blast tore at his left side. The shrapnel ripped through the left side of Carl's body like a buzzing chainsaw. I felt the extreme pressure from the blast and the fierce pain that came after.

A mixture of blood, meat, and bone sprayed, filling the air with a red mist. There was no time to think as I experienced the mind-numbing pain that shot through Carl's body. It felt as if Carl was on fire, yet no flames clung to his shredded body. As Carl screamed for his life, I noticed that the sun's rays beamed through the soft billowing clouds from above. I focused on the soothing glow of the ring. It seemed to ease the suffering I felt from the soldier.

Carl grimaced with agony, his eyes fixed on the heavenly beams of sunlight. As tears streamed down his face, he heard the soft, nurturing voice of a woman float across the searing desert wind.

She said, "Smile Carl, just remember to smile."

The sky turned bleach-white as Carl's mind slipped in and out of consciousness. The blurred images of the faces of rescue personnel trailed by as Carl's body thrashed in anguish. A swirl of golden beams pulled at my mind, beckoning me out of Carl's body. The comfort I felt within the golden rays was astonishing. I wanted to bask in the glow of this solace, but I knew that it had to end. In that moment of deep peace, I had experienced the comforting time of Carl's near death.

I realized then that when I journeyed back in time to witness people's tragedies, it was their souls that I attached to, transporting me to the most traumatic times in their lives.

I felt the cords that attached Carl's soul to the earthly plane tighten as the golden swirl slowly backtracked into the sky. His soul was lowered through the clouds and into a large green tent. As he descended toward a cold, white table, I saw Carl's ravaged body. His entire left side had been blown off, leaving only shredded muscle entangled with veins and arteries.

I felt nauseous and exhausted at the sight of this chaos, but my eyes were transfixed on the panic that ensued below me. Bright lights sheathed Carl's battered body. People in white scrubs and blue facemasks rushed around him. One of them yelled, "He's coming to!" while another medic barked, "Suture that artery!"

I was astounded as I watched the operation unfold. Carl's wounds slowly stopped seeping blood and the left side of his body was gradually stapled shut, stitches zigzagging serpentine pathways all over his side. The darkness encased me for what seemed like an eternity. Although I winced at the thought of the painful recovery Carl had in store, I anticipated the moment Carl's eyes would open once again. His heart beat like some distant drummer, hands slapping cowhide, echoing across hills and diving deep within the valleys of his spirit.

The murmuring sounds of people filled the space that I seemed to occupy, deep within Carl's soul. I realized he was coming out of his comatose state when I heard his bass voice mumble something incoherent. It seemed as though I were peering out of a slowly opening blind as the light of day filled my eyes.

The hospital room had that typical bleach-white look, everything so stark and void of feeling. A young nurse seemed to glide by, peering down at a clipboard. Her eyes slowly looked up from the folded papers and her mouth opened wide with surprise as she noticed that Carl was awake.

"Oh my! You're with us?" the nurse gasped. Then she quickly scurried off, yelling for the doctor.

Carl's eyes shut, and the outside world faded. Within seconds, his lids cracked open again. The doctor lifted Carl's eyelids, blinding light piercing Carl's sensitive retinas.

"Welcome back, Private!" the doctor said with a happy bounce in his voice.

Although it had only been a brief moment since I had begun my journey into Carl's past, it seemed like days. I felt his exhaustion as he started his physical therapy program. Carl went in and out of despair as he grappled with his plight. He suffered the most at night, with bombs blasting in his head and the screams of the fallen soldier that he barely saved echoing in his dreams.

Most every night Carl would awaken to sweat-soaked bed sheets, crying out for help. He would curse the day he was born as he stared at his limbless left side. I listened to his thoughts as they amplified throughout the corners of his mind.

He would say, "How can I live with this body?" and "What kind of life can I live if I'm an invalid? Why didn't I just die out there?"

At one point, Carl stopped eating. All food resembled flesh and blood. His depression had gotten hold of him, and he just wanted to wither away in the hospital bed. He felt dull and hopeless as he watched the sun rise and reach its midday summit, then sink behind the brown hills until darkness again captured the evening sky.

One night as Carl drifted into sleep, he noticed a glowing orb of light just outside the window next to his bed. The orb passed through the window and hovered near him as he stared wide eyed, entranced by its presence. The orb, now poised over Carl's head, radiated a golden light. It washed over his body in a glistening, soothing glow.

Carl felt peaceful and high, sensations he had not felt in a lifetime. His eyes rolled back and his face relaxed. His grimacing frown was replaced by a serene smile. The heavenly words he heard on the battlefield came back to him: "Smile, Carl ..."

Carl awoke to a pair of songbirds. He felt somehow different. A lightness filled him. He no longer felt imprisoned by his own body. The pain from his wounds was replaced by a warm, comforting sensation. As he thought about his tragic experience, instead of feeling rage and pain, Carl began to laugh.

Laughter not only filled Carl's body but engulfed the whole ward. Carl screamed with laughter, while the other men on the ward looked on in disbelief. They had been so used to Carl's screams of agony that the sound of such delectation truly perplexed them.

In an instant, Carl's bed was surrounded by nurses, doctors, and specialists. Carl just lay there, beaming with an inward radiance. He explained to everyone what he had experienced. The doctors could neither discredit his experience nor confirm its authenticity, so instead they just celebrated his cathartic breakthrough.

As I exited Carl's past, he began to whistle the same song that he had greeted me with. His words rang through my brain—"Been smilin' ever since"—as I rode the golden ribbons of light back to my time. I blew back into my chilled body, feet still planted in slush-covered boots, with a sense of relief and acceptance for my life and the world. I also had a better understanding of Carl's experience.

Carl was still speaking, but the look on his face told me that somehow he knew what I had just been through.

"Now, I could sit at home all day in a pile of misery, or I could get up and do something with my life. One day, I was collecting for UNICEF, and my mom told me panhandling would be a good way to get a couple of bucks for myself. Being out here gives me some kinda self-esteem, a feeling like I'm doing something for myself. So now I talk to people. I hear their stories and they hear mine. I see their tears and they see mine. We laugh together, and sometimes we even express our anger together."

A man walked by. He and Carl hugged and shared a laugh.

"Anyway," Carl continued, "I don't like complaining much. Ain't no room in this life for complaining. It's all about helping one another.

And that's why I'm here, to help others. Most people I see and talk to out here suffer from injured souls. Their bodies are fine and everything, but on the inside, they are hurting real bad."

His brow tightened, then relaxed. "I just offer them inspiration and acceptance. I think acceptance is all most people really want. And if I get a couple of George Washingtons for helping someone, great. So, for now I'll just stand here on my one leg, balanced on one crutch, held up by one arm, and I'll keep smiling. It's worked so far. I always tell people to take my smile with 'em—they may need it on a rainy day."

I told Carl how much I desperately needed to hear his story, and that I would take his advice to heart. Happiness filled me when I parted ways with Carl. His smile had made an imprint on my heart, and I would carry his story with me wherever I went. So, you could say Carl and I never did part, for he is ever present in every smile I see.

Chapter 6:
Geraldee

*Our greatest weakness lies in giving up. The most certain
way to succeed is always to try just one more time.*
—Thomas Edison

It's hard to believe that my experience with Carl only lasted one hour
and twenty-three minutes; it felt like hours, even days. I was becoming
addicted to these supernatural journeys. My curiosity took over as I
scanned the sidewalks, looking for another interview—another ride on
someone's personal rollercoaster.

My watch read 3:15 p.m. as I sat next to an empty fountain pool.
A small puddle of glossy ice had accumulated near the drain. The
reflection of a circling flock of pigeons fluttered in the pool of ice. The
flock landed around "the pigeon lady," a woman who would break open
a loaf of bread and let the gray birds eat from her lap. She would then
be engulfed in little winged bodies. This odd sight seemed to always
generate a crowd of spectators.

As I watched the loaf of bread disintegrate in the woman's lap, a
light flashed in the corner of my eye. Turning, I saw a younger dark-
skinned woman holding up jewelry to the people walking by. The
sun bounced off the shiny silver and golden chains as she waved them
around. I was drawn to this woman, as if I were beholden to talk to her.
Her hair was slightly matted, half covered by a hand-crocheted beanie.

She sat cross-legged, with a sign leaning up against her knees. It read, HOMELESS, PLEASE HELP.

As I approached her, she asked if I would like to purchase a necklace to help her get a bite to eat. I explained what I was doing and that I would pay her a couple of dollars for her story, and she agreed without hesitation.

"My name is Geraldee," she said, packing her jewelry in a plastic bag. "I was messing 'round wit drugs and the whole nine, okay, so as soon as I felt the warm sunlight upon my face, coming out of rehab, I found myself back in the dark. My sister took me into her house, her crack house. So there I was, a wannabe recovering addict, staying at a crack house. Shit, I remember coming in at night to some bad business." She rubbed her temples as if the memory made her head ache. "I was literally stumbling over bodies passed out and all fucked up 'cause they was blow crazy. Man, it was whack; they be syringes with exposed needles tossed everywhere. That time was by far the hardest for me, like being in the darkest nightmare of temptation."

Although I knew what would happen next, I still was not prepared for it. Geraldee's face protracted and rippled, all the buildings seemed to merge into one, and the sky changed from gray to purple, like an LSD flashback.

My footing gave way to the now-undulating sidewalk, the concrete turning into a liquid tidal pool of electric shockwaves, and I sank once again into the deep unknown. The sounds of the city pulsed through me, my ears filled with R&B bass beats, while the waves transformed into rotating hips and sweat-drenched thighs.

Was I being sucked into some behemoth gala, or would this turn out to be yet another bloodcurdling past life? The phantasmal journey ended with my head stuffed in a shrub, puking my guts out. As I wiped the dribble of mucus off my chin, I noticed my hand had turned dark brown and petite.

Okay, now I'm Geraldee? I thought as she stood upright, world spinning.

Her thoughts rang clear, as if she spoke over an intercom: *Goddamn, must be going through withdrawal! Ain't even been off the junk fo' three days!*

As Geraldee scanned the property, she stood in front of a large ransacked, abandoned house. The distant murmur of alto-beats thundered through cinderblocks and drywall.

Goddamn, what now? Geraldee thought, frustration filling her mind.

As she approached the front door, a foul odor filled the air, like rotting garbage. The door had been knocked off its hinges and then wired up with bundles of twist ties. As it fell open, a wafting stench escaped, followed by a swarm of flies. The floor seemed to move as Geraldee continued forward.

The ground was laden with people, shaking and moaning. Every footfall was followed by the sound of breaking glass. Syringes covered the walls, their needles jabbed into the stained, peeling wallpaper. The only illumination came from lighter sparks, along with a soft glow emanating from crack pipes.

"Sh-Sherell, where are you?" Geraldee whispered, her voice now trembling with fear.

It was a tour through a house of horrors, and I wondered what would pop out from every corner, preparing for some gruesome sight. I came to a room where a candle wildly flickered, casting spirit-dancers on the wall. The room was filled with couples fiercely copulating, their buttocks glistening with passion-fire as they yowled.

The room seemed to boil with lust as Geraldee watched, her horror quickly turning amatory. Dizziness took over. Her skin dripped with sweat, like the lone candle as it hypnotized its audience.

In the middle of this orgy, Geraldee noticed a familiar face. I automatically knew it was her cousin Sherell. Sherell straddled a large black man. His tight muscles glowed in the candlelight, like hematite on fire. They slammed their bodies together as if to evict, or call in, some wild demon. Sherell glanced at Geraldee as her head bobbed forth and back. She began to cackle like a possessed coyote, taunting its prey.

Geraldee held her ears tight. Her cousin's insane laughter seemed to burrow deep into her brain. She dropped to her knees, pleading to Sherell to stop her madness, but her pleas just made things worse.

"Why are you doing this?" Geraldee screamed as she gripped the doorway.

Sherell, now riding the man cowgirl style, raised her arms in the air and pointed to Geraldee. She yelled, "You never could handle no heat, could you, Geral!"

Sherell slid her hand down to her crotch, her dark bush glistening with passion juices. Her hand slowly emerged, cream covering her fingertips.

"Here," she shrieked, as she flicked her fingers, "have some frosting!"

Sherell flung her juices at Geraldee. They sparkled like pearls in the night sky as they whizzed through the air. The cream landed on the tip of Geraldee's nose and on her right cheek. Geraldee gasped in disbelief. She knew her cousin got crazy from time to time, but this was demented.

Geraldee was humiliated. The one person in the world whom she could trust had just turned on her, stuck a rusty blade into her back, and then beat her to the ground.

"Get yo ashy feet out my kitchen girl!" Sherell roared, her voice deep, as if she were about to transform into some killer beast.

Geraldee spun around and rushed toward the front door. She stumbled over squirming bodies, falling on top of their foulness. She felt the dark presence of death, as if some of the people she fell on had already expired. Geraldee flew out the front door, weeping in humiliation.

"Oh Lord, what am I gonna do now?" she cried as she crouched, knees scraping the ground.

I could hear mad laughter coming from inside the house, as if Sherell had some sort of spell over the inhabitants. Geraldee limped off into the darkness, defeated and sobbing with heartache.

I flew out of Geraldee's past, relieved that my time was up. My body relaxed as I was swept back to my time. I felt fatigued as I landed on the sidewalk, reorienting myself to the present time. Geraldee spoke slowly.

"So, there I was, once again, surrounded by drugs and alcohol and nowhere to breeze to."

Geraldee's cries reverberated in my mind as she spoke.

"There was confusion around every corner. I was at my breaking point, when I discovered a halfway house. I found my sanctuary in the midst of all that madness. I got seven months clean now."

Geraldee's face turned sunny.

"It's powerful and it's workin'. Like slipping into a fresh new pair of jeans. My soul has finally found its home."

She opened her coat and flapped her arms, pretending to fly.

I began to feel lightheaded. Images cartwheeled through my mind, throwing me off balance. I envisioned a roomful of people with Geraldee in the center of the crowd. Everyone hugged and patted Geraldee on the back. It was a celebration of her sobriety. The images in my head cleared as I sat down on the cold concrete bench. Geraldee asked if I was feeling okay. I assured her that I was just tired.

"But it ain't easy. No sir. It's hard work! Like building a new house. Every now and again I'll pass a street corner, in the old hood where I used to score, and the pull of this disease will nag at me. Sometimes, I'll bump into someone I used to run with and they be like: 'Hey, Gera! You wanna party?' And I say, 'Naw, ain't messin' wit it no more. It be dead and stinkin'!' Or I just pass by and pay 'em no mind."

Geraldee raised her head. I could tell she felt empowered.

"So, I'm off the streets now with a roof over my head. Sacrifices have been made: some that were hard, like not hanging wit the old crew, and some that were easier, like having a curfew. Late nights is on the weekends. But it's all worth it, you know, bein' clean and all."

A leftover image of Geraldee flickered in my head. She lay in a bed with serenity on her face. I could feel the satisfaction of her present condition. She had found the stability that she had longed for all her life. She slept peacefully, knowing the nightmare was over and her path toward healing had just begun.

"There ain't nothin' for me on the streets no how," Geraldee continued with honor in her voice.

"The streets is dead to me now, like that dead bird over there." She nodded in the direction of a bird, belly up and frozen to the sidewalk.

"Flies and maggots be eatin' away at it. Well, I ain't no dead bird or filthy maggot no more. I'm on the right track now. Amen."

Geraldee rushed off. It was dinnertime at the halfway house and she didn't want to be late. I chased her down, having forgotten to give her the two dollars I owed her. She thanked me, gratitude written on her face, and then scampered off.

I had done enough for the day. I had experienced another war, been through a house of dread, and weathered gut-wrenching abuse. It was time to process all this derangement, to retreat to my warm home, away from the madness of the streets.

Chapter 7:
Dennis

Much violence is based on the illusion that life is a property to be defended and not to be shared.
—Henri Nonwen

After one of the most peaceful sleeps I'd had in a great many nights, I was eager to hit the streets again and document a few more courageous stories. I spent a better part of the morning going through my notes and listening to a few stories to make sure they were all audible. After a filling brunch, I headed out.

Sunday morning in the city is a peaceful time. Church sonance reverberates through alleyways. The streets take refuge from the endless supply of traffic. It seemed as if the very sidewalk I treaded on was soft and relaxed.

I discovered that finding a good interview was like stumbling upon a fishing hole loaded with big, hungry fish. The best place to find a good story was at the mission, where homeless people frequented. It was there that I found my next subject, sitting at a table by himself, reading a newspaper. As I approached the tall, thin, brown-skinned man, he slowly lowered his paper and fashioned a friendly smile.

"Are you the guy who's going around taping people's stories?" he said as he took a laggard drag on his cigarette.

"Yes, that's me. Would you like to take part?" I said eagerly.

"What's in it for me?" he said, suspicion glazing his wide eyes.

I explained that the project was mainly for my own growth, and that if it ever became a book, its purpose would be to educate the public on the homeless condition in this country.

He smiled wide and giggled like an innocent child. "I was just testing you. Of course I'll contribute!"

He invited me over to his table and sat back.

"You know, word's getting around that you are working the streets for interviews?" he said, as if I were some kind of celebrity.

I took a deep breath, not sure if this was a good thing, or if this project was getting to be too intense. After all, I only expected a few interviews, just enough to raise my own awareness.

"My name is Dennis," he began. "I've been out on the streets for two months, almost three. I was a respiratory therapist. I have an associate's degree in science and was working in a nursing home as a boarder legal. Had to pay child support, pay rent, buy a car, *and* live in this society.

"So, there I was—got my last pay check, took my dog, went to the bus station, and then I got robbed. Actually, to be honest with you, I got mugged. I made the mistake in going down to the bus depot at 2:00 a.m. That's when that place turns from G-rated to R-rated. It was a two-man outfit that robbed me, one in front and one from behind. This one guy, real clean and all, comes up t—"

Before Dennis could complete his sentence, my ride had already begun. To my surprised relief, I was more in control of the journey, like a racecar driver who just learned to hold the reins of his vehicle. I mastered the dizziness and subdued the overwhelming sensations of my mind, body, and spirit.

This time, I felt as if I had taken a hallucinogenic drug. The room began to turn wavy. My body followed, as I rode the waves like some cosmic surfer. The giant funnel spat me out onto a cold tile floor. I lifted my head to see a large neon sign that read CITY BUS STATION.

The station was vacant. All the seats were empty and the florescent lights flickered overhead. As I got up on my feet, I noticed a single person sitting a few yards away from where I stood. That had to be Dennis, the man I was interviewing.

As I came within hailing distance, I felt a familiar pull at my flesh. Before I had the chance to blink, I realized that I was being sucked into the man's body.

Inhabiting another person's body is almost like waking up to a dead arm—no control, just dead weight, a phantom limb.

I did not notice the two large men approach Dennis from behind. They must not have had any shoes on. I knew that he was going to be attacked, but nothing could prepare me for the blow that came next. Dennis was bludgeoned with a hard object, maybe a baseball bat or a two-by-four. I felt the impact with each jarring blow.

The percussive blasts resounded through Dennis's body as he begged for the muggers to stop. His left forearm pulsed. Fierce pain had taken over, and the room lifted, spinning my mind until I became nauseous. I tried to separate myself from the agony Dennis was experiencing but could not tear myself from the trancelike state that I was in.

Dennis lay spread eagle, gazing at the stained ceiling tiles, thoughts scrambling through his confused mind, trying to take refuge in the memories of better times. The waves of searing pain locked him into that terrible moment. Tears of frustration streamed down his face, dropping in salty puddles on the soiled floor. He was so close to escaping the city that had held him hostage, so close to starting new, but the frigid realization that his sentence was not yet up filled his mind. There was no escape.

Dennis's wallet lay next to him, its contents scattered around him, silhouetting his battered head. He rolled over, fumbling for the wallet, only to find all his savings had been snatched.

"No!" Dennis yelled, throwing the empty billfold across the room. It flapped through the air like a frantic bird.

Thunderous footfalls scrambled toward Dennis, while hurried voices dispatched EMTs to the scene. Just as Dennis attempted to speak to an officer, I turned cold and began to feel a pull from the unknown. The room disintegrated into a zillion pieces.

While I floated through the abyss, Dennis's voice echoed in my mind.

As my eyes focused on the serpentine smoke swirls from the lone cigarette, squished in its ashtray grave, I realized I had returned to the present time. Dennis seemed to be voicing his frustrations as his voice roared, demanding justice. His passion sobered my bemused mind as I sat in attention.

Dennis continued, lecturing like a professor, "Even the organizations set up to help the homeless are under the perception that all homeless are drug addicts, and if you are not an addict you can't get any help. We live in an extreme society, where if you are not completely at your last ropes, there's no help for you."

Dennis spoke with such exactitude that I became lost in his words.

"You can't get into any programs and there's not any housing unless you have a job. There are lots of hospitals around here, so maybe I'll get lucky and find that job."

He gazed out the smutted window and over the rooftops, as if searching for the hospital he spoke of.

"A lot of the guys that I've talked to out here are victims of their circumstances. The majority are addicts in one way or another. There are doctors, lawyers, schoolteachers, dentists, and city workers out here."

Images of working-class professionals, people I encountered every day, flipped through my mind like a cartoonist's sketchbook as Dennis continued.

"Families, veterans, social workers, and police officers walk these streets. The blood of America is out here on the skids, neglected, pushed aside, and forgotten."

The room seemed to exhaust all oxygen as I tried to breathe. I coughed, lungs reaching for air, tongue clapping, while the people Dennis spoke of marched through my mind. The crowd mounted, like some kind of black mold, filling the streets, covering everything. Anxiety stuffed my gut, as if the infestation had reached me and taken over my whole body.

When I came to, Dennis was rubbing my back, his voice now soft to my ears.

"I'm so sorry," he said. "I sometimes get a little intense when I speak about the streets."

I assured him that my sickly state had nothing to do with his story, but was instead due to a lack of sleep. Dennis sat down again, concern still present in his eyes.

"We can't force-feed anything to anyone," he said. "I'm a Christian that respects other people, but there are people out here that try to cram their beliefs down other people's throats. That don't work; it just causes fear. Fear is what brought a lot of people out here to begin with. Something just snapped inside them, and before they knew it, they were standing in a soup kitchen line.

"One more thing," Dennis said with urgency. "We ain't all bad, you know, homeless people. We are just going through our life experience. People make judgments; they say that we are all not up to scratch, dirty and crooked. They need to open their eyes to reality, and the reality is that America is homeless."

Dennis shook my hand. The firmness told me he appreciated my efforts. He left me sitting alone at the table, staring through the window, just as he had done, searching for the next street to journey down.

There was so much more I needed to know, so many more questions I needed to answer. And I knew that the tangled roads below would bring me the harvest of answers I was looking for.

Chapter 8:
Charles

Just 'cause you got the monkey off your back, doesn't mean the circus has left town.

—George Carlin

As I walked the narrow alleyways hunting down my next interview, hours passed and I began to feel dizzy. My quest had turned into an addiction. I had to have another cathartic experience at any cost. My legs turned to rubber from hoofing the seemingly colossal hills, and my feet burned from hours of trekking on hard cobblestone paths.

I sat on the steps of City Hall, head between my legs, world spinning out of control. I imagined a white flag flying high above the buzzing city, flapping with urgency. I had surrendered, and I decided to turn my quest over to the universe.

As I sat on the hard stone steps, my eye caught an advertisement on a bus. It went something like this: *What is, is. What isn't, isn't. You become so obsessed with what isn't that you miss what is.*

I was awestruck by this profound message, and, what's more, how much I really needed that wisdom. As I sat up erect, mouth wide open, I heard a voice.

"Man, you look like you seen a ghost!" the man sitting next to me said, as he munched on a hotdog.

"No," I said, wiping the sweat from my brow, "I just saw something that gave me a much-needed boost."

The man appeared to be a street person. His clothes looked as if they hadn't been washed in some time and his skin looked leathery in the late afternoon sun.

"Not all people is homeless from drugs and alcohol you know," he said, as if anticipating I would ask for his story. I asked him if I could tape what he had to say and he agreed.

"Some are on Social Security," he continued, "and can't afford to pay rent. And then there are the folks who are drug users. One guy is even a nurse. Now, I don't know all their stories, but I can speak from my own experience."

The man's long, matted beard gave him the appearance of a guru. His stained white shirt lifted in the gentle breeze. He smiled at the sky, taking in a deep breath. When he spoke, the holy persona that I had invested him with evaporated and he reverted into an ordinary man. He was prosaic as the words slurred from his toothless mouth.

"Name's Charles, and I've been struggling with drug and alcohol abuse for over twenty years now. Man, I'm tellin' you, it ain't easy!"

Charles tossed a ketchup-and-mustard-stained napkin in the trash. He made a "swooshing" sound when the trash disappeared into the can.

He went on, "Been tryin' to get into the program upstairs."

He pointed to the Salvation Army building across the street.

"And God willing, I'll get there. But I don't want to serve a twenty-year sentence on the streets like some of these guys. I mean, I've only been out here for eight and I want more than this. But as long as I mess with the blow and the booze, I will never have more."

My body began to rise, but this time, my journey to the other side was more of an intuitive flash than a mind-bending transcendental ride. I visualized Charles huddled under the creamy glow of a neon sign. It read, THE FUZZY GRAPE GENTLEMEN'S CLUB. His body churned and quaked as the evening crowd poured through the front doors.

As I came back into my body, I shook off this latest vision, while Charles continued to talk.

"Man, I did some jacked-up shit back in the day. Damn, I even did a little pimpin'! I had me a couple-a ho's. They doubled as shakers at a booty club and we was doin' fine for a time. But it all went gutter, as soon as I started using."

We moved to a nearby bus stop bench after a policeman asked us to vacate the steps. This agitated Charles.

"Man, all I ever want is respect, but seems like the cops just be dissin' us homeless folks. They don't see past the rags and into the soul. It's just an ego trip to them. I made Dean's list in high school," he went on, "and went to community college. I'm no fool and there's no excuse for me being homeless. Well, I could say the coke brought me here, but that's a cop-out. All the money that I made went straight up my nose. But I do want out of this hell.

"Man, once you been out here for a time even your lingo changes. You know, I didn't always talk like this. The streets change you."

I could tell Charles was trying to change his dialect. A noticeable effort in the pronunciation of each word could be heard.

"I'm sitting here in limbo with my hand out until I can stand on my own."

Charles changed his posture, holding his head high.

"I eat three squares a day, seven days a week, thanks to charities such as the Salvation Army. There are places to go, you just have to reach out.

"It's amazing how many people are homeless. I mean, I never really noticed how many people is doin' bad 'til I came here. You would never think that so many people are so bad off, other than drug addicts, not in 'this country.' It's unbelievable how long the lines run with all kinds of people, and it's dangerous too. People come down here just lookin' for trouble. Sometimes you have to grow an eye in the back of your head."

Charles scanned the streets. It seemed that just the thought of an attack put him on full alert. I began to feel the pressure emanating from him. The air fell heavy around us. The thunderous treble of a car stereo broke the nervous silence as Charles continued.

"You can't force anyone to get their life back together. People have to admit that they are powerless over their situation; they need to reach out. A lot of people say that they aren't able to get any help, but they just ain't ready."

His voice turned mellow, as if he had just admitted his own powerlessness.

"So now I'm dependent on someone else to take care of me. Now that's a big blow from Big Brother. Some people abuse the system, while the others are genuinely in a rut. I've met a few people who have climbed out of their personal ruts, so there is hope.

"And then there are the people who are suffering from mental illness. They ain't doin' no drugs. They just caught up in their own mental suffering—that's frightening to me. They be walking around in a daze, in mental anguish, not knowing where they are. I'm like that when I'm on coke, but I eventually come down. Without medication, they are always gone.

"I've always been selfish when it came to drugs. I mean I always thought that I was hurting only myself. Didn't realize that I was leaving a lot of casualties behind, you know, family, friends, acquaintances. I have no one now. Only myself, and I ain't myself's best friend.

"So I've got to make friends with myself before I do anything else. Like my mother used to say: 'You take care of your own backyard and then you worry about the others.' I hope I don't let you down mom."

He looked at me. "You think that was a good ending?" he said with concern in his eyes.

I assured him that it was a unique and powerful ending and that many people would relate to it. He smiled, gums protruding, and thanked me for my willingness to listen to him.

I couldn't help but feel hopeful for Charles as he walked across the street and into the Salvation Army building. It was as if our talk had given him the boost he needed to go upstairs, to seek out that much-needed support to climb out of his rut. I wished him well on his new journey, and then continued on mine.

Chapter 9:
Eddie

Content makes poor men rich; discontentment makes rich men poor.

—Benjamin Franklin

I hadn't walked a hundred yards before I found my next subject. He stood leaning against a trashcan, his layered clothing flapping in the cool breeze. I asked him for an interview immediately and was surprised at how willing he was to bare his soul to me.

"Sure, what the hell. Got no one else to talk to, 'cept this here garbage can," he said. "Quit school, dropped out in the eleventh grade. Man, I wasn't interested in their bullshit lessons! Most of it was crap anyway. So one day, in the middle of class actually, I just up and left, just like that! And I didn't return. Way I looks at it, is if I don't get respect, none will be given from me, dig?

"Got married, got divorced. She found somebody she liked better. Man, I don't blame her! Shoot, I was a damn loudmouth drunk. Coming home half-licked, spittin' and-a sputterin' all kinda freaky shit. So, when she left, I wasn't too surprised. That don't mean I don't miss her though. Life spiraled, and then, well, here I am standing on Fifth and Eighth panhandling my way through life—at the moment, that is."

He patted the pavement as if it were a sentient being, almost as if he had domesticated the ground on which we stood.

"Damn, man, do you realize that this whole thang you doin' right now is bringin' back old pains?" He pointed to my tape recorder. "Ain't nobody done squeezed out this shit in years, and here you come along just tappin' right into me, like some holy-rollin' healer."

He looked at me with wild jester's eyes, head cocked back as if he were about to strike, like a stirred cobra.

"But you ain't the enemy. Naw, you just a surveyor, curious 'bout life, ain't ya?"

I wasn't sure how to answer this, but as he continued his story, I began to feel more comfortable, like I was winning him over. We sat on two overturned oil drums next to a gyro stand. His shopping cart sat next to him, filled with all of his belongings.

"Anyway," he went on, "my name is Edward, but you can call me Eddie, and you can say I's born to be on this side of the tracks."

Eddie drew a rough line in the dirt with a trashed antenna.

"See, we is on this side of the line, and they, the well-ta-do's, is on that side." He whipped the broken antenna at the ground.

My shades began to fog up, and the air around me dropped in temperature. That old familiar dizziness returned, spinning my body until I blacked out. When I came to, I was dressed in a mauve leisure suit with hands the color of cork.

Eddie stood facing a large bank building. He was inebriated, arms swinging like swords cutting through the air.

"You pigs!" he shouted at the empty bank windows. "Don't you know who I am?"

Eddie lowered his voice to a growl. "Why, I'm the lord of this here city, and I demand my money!"

A well-dressed man wearing a three-piece suit, hair slicked back, holding a walkie-talkie, emerged from the front doors.

"Mr. Owens, they told you," he said, sounding out each word, "you-cannot-take-out-a-loan-here. Your credit is no good!"

Eddie raised his head toward the man. His eyes burned like embers.

"You too good for my business? I been to every bank in this sleaze-pit of a town and none of y'all will take my business. I just want to open shop. Can't you just—?"

Two security guards approached him from either side. Eddie squatted down and picked up his briefcase and began swinging it around like a Samurai sword.

As the guards moved closer to Eddie, he swung more fiercely. I could feel his heart pounding. He began to sweat profusely under his polyester suit and his vision blurred. The guard to his left stealthily approached. Eddie's case dipped suddenly, hitting the man in the neck. The guard let out a gasp and spun to the ground.

The injured man lay on the ground holding his neck while the other guard unsheathed his club. Eddie looked at the fallen guard. He was shocked by what he had done and wanted to apologize to the man. While Eddie was distracted by this, the guard to his right prepared to strike.

The blow from the guard's baton barreled into Eddie's shoulder, spinning him around. Eddie held up his briefcase to block the other blows. The guard let loose multiple strikes and Eddie blocked each of them with his case. The pounding of metal against leather echoed through the streets and attracted the attention of nearby pedestrians.

A crowd formed around the three men to watch the sideshow. Eddie stumbled back, losing his balance, and fell hard against the pavement. He held the case over his face as the guard whaled on his legs, rendering Eddie senseless.

As he was carried into the ambulance, restrained to a gurney, Eddie yelled out to the crowd, "They're crooks and cowards! I'm the victim here! I am the victim!"

The people in the crowd looked on in bewilderment. Some held their mouths, while others stood entranced by the whole event.

As the camera crew and reporters arrived, I disappeared into the bright flashes of cameras and the murmur of the crowd. The heat of the city dissipated as I vanished into nothingness, my body merging with time and space. I sensed the winter chill as I approached my present time and prepared for landing.

"But anyway, on the real," he continued. "I's never did feel right 'round them rich folk no how. I'm a man of the streets and the streets really haven't been too bad to me. I done did a lot of things that was outta pocket, and I've paid for most of that, but I can't say that I'm a wretched dude neither. I believe I have earned the respect of the streets and on the flip as well.

"You know that you can track down some of the most off-the-hook people out here? I mean like, there be artists, poets, and architects out here, and if you lucky, you may run into a few geniuses.

"There's this one cat," Eddie cocked his head back, smiling at the sky, "who lives under Fourth Street, man! Mapped out the universe deep inside his little nook beneath the bridge. Yah, you'd get a lot outta him!"

Eddie paused for a moment as if his mind froze, thinking about some deep memory from his past life. A child laughed in the distance. He continued, "I had me one of those, a child that is. Her name was Sharleen. She was so beautiful, but I had to split. There was no way I could drag her down in this here tide pool. I never did graduate from nothin', never did have no degree, nothin' sayin' I was good enough to share in the riches of the world. All my friends who I used to think were from the same rib took off runnin' when they saw I was street bound. One tried to help, but it was too late.

"So, here I am! What can I do but live day to day and be thankful for the breath in my lungs."

Eddie sighed. He relaxed his shoulders and shook his head as if he were forgiving himself for his sins. He smiled as he looked toward the sinking sun.

"Can't wait 'til the spring. Everything is fresh and growing stronger. All the flowers be peepin' at ya. The womens be dressin' all fly 'n all. Makes me wanna start new. Maybe I'll be stronger too, and maybe then I'll graduate from the streets.

"Gots to go brotha," Eddie said as he tugged on his packed cart. "Got places to go and grub to eat! Keep up the learnin'. You doin' a good thang, my man. Maybe someday I'll see your book on a shelf somewhere."

And that was it. Eddie's interview was finished. Soon after he vanished from view, I picked myself up and headed home. It had been a long, eventful day and I could feel sleep closing in.

As I followed the setting sun south toward my home, I pondered the day's journeys. I thought about how resourceful and courageous the people that I had interviewed were. All eight of their faces flashed through my mind, like a cartoon flip-page. Their stories seemed so fantastical, yet I knew they were all real. After all, I had experienced every word for myself.

Chapter 10:
K. W. P.

Current statistics estimate that more than 299,000 veterans are homeless on any given night. And, more than 500,000 experience homelessness over the course of a year.

—from nextstageinc.org

The next morning I was in a fog. School had totally slipped away from me. I had an incomplete project to turn in, and my mind was spinning from a barrage of images of despair and valiancy. I was so engrossed in the lives of other people that I had forgotten my own obligations. By now the ring on my left index finger was a part of me, like some growth that had taken over my life.

I decided to slap together my design and turn it in as it was. I tried to explain my fantastical side project to my teacher, but, as expected, he remarked, "This is a design school, not a school for writers. Get it together!"

I left school that day with my confidence level dwindling, whimpering like a beaten-down old dog. The semester was almost complete and I had fallen behind on two important projects. The heat had been cranked up, and I could clearly feel the burn.

Determined to make it home and finish other school projects, I made a sudden detour past my favorite panhandler spots. As my snow-covered car came into view, a man caught my eye, and although I tried my hardest to resist, I could not resist the urge to approach him for an interview.

"One interview won't hurt. I mean, I did four yesterday!" I thought as I approached the bundled-up man. He looked a bit like a former member of Bob Marley and the Wailers, with his long, snakelike dreadlocks dangling over his coat collar. He glanced at me with suspicious, coal dark eyes.

The closer I got to this man, the more he seemed to try to avoid me, as if he knew what I was about to ask him. Perhaps I had been spoiled by the other "easier" interviews that this now seemed like a challenge, maybe even a rejection. I approached with caution, making eye contact as I got close.

My introduction was a bit shaky. The two scars on his face unsettled me. I could tell he felt my nervousness as I stood there, tongue-tying every one of my words. But he said nothing, as if he were deep in thought.

"You say this is for a kinda educational project?" he said, deadpan, like some Zen master.

"Yeah, I'm seeking out answers to get a better understanding of the homelessness problem—"

He cut me off before I could finish. "You mean, like you're doing this for your own education?"

I saw interest developing in his eyes.

"Yes, but I may decide someday to incorporate the stories I've collected into a book," I said.

He shook his head and grinned, as if he had just been given an insight from some invisible force.

"Yeah, I gotcha," he said as he pulled out a hand-rolled cigarette. "Name's K. W. P. You can call me K. P. for short, and, well, I got some things to say. Not sure if you'll want to use it or not."

He seemed to have very little confidence, but I could tell he had a story to tell. So I gave him a dollar, all I had in my wallet, and he began his account.

"I was in the Navy, a SEAL to be exact, and served my country for eight years. I was just shy of making lieutenant junior grade when I got sick. It turned out my mind couldn't handle the pressure anymore. I was even getting jump pay—that's when a soldier gets paid extra for being in dangerous situations. Man, the training was like being in a war. You see these scars?" He pointed to the pale raised wounds on his face. "They just from basic training, so you can imagine what life was like in the field. While in training, we had to dive for weights in clouded water while blindfolded, with our hands and legs tied. I had to use my mouth to bring the ten-pound weights to the surface. And if I came up empty, I would get whipped with some sort of cord. That's where this one came from." He pointed to a scar on the bridge of his nose.

I became fixed on K. P.'s story. His words were like a rope that lassoed my mind, yanking my soul out of my body. The winter chill no longer tormented me as I was hurled into another dimension. I then landed hard against a sand dune, knowing I had arrived at my destination. From the sound of things, it wasn't going to be a joyride.

I was unable to visualize anything, but the grittiness in my mouth and inbetween my toes made me aware that I was on a beach somewhere. I could taste the salty air as I stumbled in circles, but with a blindfold tightly bound around my head and my hands tied behind my back, I felt helpless in this new environment. I had to find a way to relax and just let K. P.'s body guide me around this place.

The popping of gunfire rang in my ears, throwing off K. P.'s gait. His muscles convulsed after each jarring burst, until he collapsed. As he lay on the cool sand, I heard the sound of approaching footfalls. Pungent cigar smoke filled the air.

When a boot hammers into your gut, the world around you disappears and is replaced with a torch of pain. That's what happened next. I don't know where it came from, but the steel toe of a military-issue boot landed square in K. P.'s midsection.

"Get up, you pansy-ass mamma's boy!" a voice from hell screamed into K. P.'s ear. "This ain't no Holiday Inn! Are you givin' up on me, soldier?"

Then all of the sounds were muted, and the world went to sleep.

When K. P.'s eyes opened, he was in a cage submerged in a foot of water. He coughed uncontrollably, having inhaled some of the murky water, and shook wildly. The cage seemed to bend in on itself as K. P. focused on his new surroundings.

"Ah shit!" he screamed, realizing his predicament.

"Don't you worry," a voice from the other side of the room whispered. "This is all a part of the training. It'll be over soon."

The comforting voice came from another cage, but he could not see the other prisoner. He could only hear his calm voice.

"So this is all part of our training?" K. P. said as he lifted himself onto a wooden platform a couple of inches above the stagnant water.

"That's right. They just want to toughen us up," the man said in a hypnotic tone.

I could feel confusion building inside K. P.'s tired mind. It felt as if he just wanted to end the whole charade but was helpless in his iron pen. Then the man spoke again, this time with a much more urgent tone.

"You know time is running out, don't you?" the man said, as if he were drilling K. P.

"What? What do you mean, 'time is running out'?"

"The world's on fire and you got the extinguisher, so what are you going to do about it?"

The man's voice mellowed again, but that didn't make things any better. K. P. just became more confused.

"Well," K. P. said, "I'll put out the fire."

The other man began to laugh. At first the laughter emerged in a titter, and then it rose to a crescendo of cackles. I had no idea what was happening, whether this was a part of the training or a form of punishment. The laughter filled every corner of the large dark room, while K. P. held his ears tight. The hornlike laughter began to make K. P. sick to his gut, until he threw up through the bars of the cage. The force of the vomit sprayed around the cage, making the unseen man's laughter even stronger.

"Stop it," K. P. moaned, "stop this madness!"

K. P. began to yell, but his bellows were drowned out by the high decibels of laughter.

The laughter stopped. The silence that followed was even more maddening than the clamor.

K. P.'s ears perked to the sound of a creaky door. It was the cage of the invisible man. A shadow emerged from the silhouetted metal box, then seemed to float toward K. P. and stop, hovering four feet from the coop. K. P. answered dozens of maddening questions, while he went in and out of consciousness. The cage seemed to undulate, as if it were a living, breathing creature. I could feel sores developing on K. P.'s flesh from the constant moisture.

"You did it, soldier!" a voice barked loudly, jolting K. P. awake.

"Wha-what?" K. P. said, baffled at the shadow's words.

"Forty-nine hours, fifty-two minutes, and thirty-two seconds— that's how long you've been in here!"

The voice now sounded upbeat, conveying a strong vote of confidence. "And not once did you utter the words, 'Mommy, I want to go home!'"

The jangling of keys filled the air, followed by a hollow "click," and the door to K. P.'s freedom creaked open. A wave of fluorescent lights streamed through a sizable warehouse. A large man in mud-covered fatigues stood in front of K. P. He loomed over him, half-smiling at the spent soldier.

"S-sir ... wh-what's going on?" K. P. asked.

"Yer free ta go is what's goin' on, soldier!" the man said, drool sprinkles landing on K. P.'s forehead. "You passed this segment of yer training! Congratulations!"

The menacing man towered over K. P. The veins in his forehead popped out, making him appear monstrous in the flickering yellow lights. He shook K. P.'s hand, and two of his knuckles popped under the pressure of the man's grip.

I flew from K. P.'s training grounds, leaving him on his knees sobbing in the muck. The warehouse was in fact very big, located in the middle of a military training camp. As my transparent self was lowered back into my present, bundled-up body, I struggled to fix my concentration on K. P.'s current story.

"When I got out, I felt like I was going back to war."

K. P. looked and sounded like an entirely different person, as if he had been stripped clean of any confidence he may have once had.

"Couldn't get no work at all. I tried real hard, but there was no way in hell, nobody was hiring. All that was hiring was back overseas."

I tried asking about this, but K. P. would not answer any of my questions. Instead, he ignored me and seemed to lecture to an invisible crowd. He appeared unaffected by the frigid winter winds as he unzipped his down-filled coat. So I decided to lean up against the parking lot's chain-link fence, recorder pointed at K. P.'s mouth, and let his story unfold.

"Like I said," he went on, "I was in the SEALs during some of the Iraq war. I got a GED but no other education, so what I learned I learned in the Navy. When I went for interviews, it was like they assumed right off the bat that I wasn't right for the job. Man, my head was spinning from all the doors that slammed in my face."

As I stood there, legs locked, shoulder pressed up against the waffle-iron fencing, I imagined how frustrated I would be in his position. Coming home after serving my country to find no support, only scars and twisted war memories. I knew deep down that a part of what K. P. needed was someone to listen to his story. He seemed to open more pages of his account as I continued to listen.

"Now, the hardest part of all this is the winters. Just keeping warm is a struggle. I spend most of my nights finding that warm spot. I've slept on vents from buildings, in doorways, abandoned cars and dumpsters. I've slept in burnt-out buildings, under bridges, and in spillways. I've slept in subway halls, public restrooms, and in cardboard boxes. You have to be willing to turn into a rat to survive sometimes. Some people make it. Some people don't."

It seemed like K. P. was preparing for a eulogy as he cleared his throat and arched his back. His eyes connected with mine. I leveled my recorder and nodded to K. P., giving him the go-ahead, and he resumed.

"One night, okay, it's the dead of winter, right? There's this huge blizzard coming in. I mean, I can see a wall of white storming into town. Now, I was trained not to panic in war, so there's no way in hell I'm doing it now! So I scan up and down the streets looking for shelter, when I see this large washer/dryer box. I walked calmly over to the box, opened it up, and noticed it was empty."

I felt K. P.'s words slip into my bloodstream, like a heroin injection, and then my mind emptied. Again, I had landed in another part of K. P.'s past, but this time I could still hear his muffled voice, as if he were speaking through the blizzard. As he moved through the deepening snow, I could feel the blustering wind pounding on him while at the same time I listened to his story unfold from a future narration.

"At this point the storm is right on me!" he said, as a wave of icy crystals exploded on me. "So I just tipped the box on its side, climbed in and sealed the flaps shut."

The box trembled from the untamed winds. K. P. braced the cardboard walls, riding out the storm.

"It was a cold and windy night, but I got a few winks, and when I woke in the morning, I realized that I was sleeping under a massive mound of snow in the middle of an alley."

K. P. plowed opened the flaps. The morning sunlight bounced off snow waves, blinding his eyes.

"So, uh, I emerged from the box, kinda like bein' born again, to a winter wonderland. Man, it was a trip!"

I slid out of K. P.'s body, zipping through the frigid air and landing back in my body. I checked my watch. An hour had passed since the interview had begun. K. P. seemed to have mellowed quite a bit and was now squatting on an upturned bucket. He spoke with a much more subdued tone as he finished his account.

"Some say the craziest of them make it. I know you've got to stretch yourself to limits you woulda never imagined to survive out here. I've been all the way down to Arizona. It's hard enough to stay in one town. I've been all around. Just got back from Jacksonville. It's been getting worse down there because they are losing their missions. So I just stick it out here."

K. P. moved to an upright position. He looked across the icy river, like a prisoner accepting his fate.

"My contacts are getting stronger—you need contacts out here. I ain't talking about the kinds you put in your eyes either. It's the friendlies, the people that help me out. You gotta get to know the people that know where the food is. The ones that know where the warm bed is. The kind of person that has an open heart, that helps me to feel that it's good to be alive. And it is good to be alive."

I was baffled by K. P.'s last statement.

It's good to be alive? I thought as I waved good-bye to his disappearing body. I was inspired by his positive outlook on life, especially after all he had been through. I pondered how much I could use a dose of his strength and determination, how I often complained about the most insignificant things.

Eric Schatz

Dancing to my car, I felt full of gratitude. My life was full, rich and abundant with possibilities. I brimmed with gratitude as I drove home, eager to tackle not only my unfinished school projects but any unfinished life challenges.

Chapter 11:
Shercy

Domestic violence is a major contributing factor to homelessness among women; perhaps 86% of homeless women were physically abused prior to life on the streets.
—Fisher, Hovel, Hofstetter, and Hough: International Journal of Health Services, 1995

Carpet foam, Exacto blades, an airbrush gun, acrylic paints, plastic googly eyes, and faux hair. My list of supplies littered the living room floor, while I stared at the pile like some voracious beast, ready to pounce. I worked through the day on my animated puppet project, making sure all the gears and mechanisms were in place, and then I tested it out.

Her name was Zebble, a cross between Animal from *The Muppet Show* and some drag-queen alien. I fashioned a remote control device inside her head to be able to control her from a distance. It would operate the mouth and the eyelids. I turned the remote controller on and the remote box in the head, held my breath, and then maneuvered the joystick.

To my amazement, Zebble came to life! Her eyes winked and her mouth flapped open, baring her pearly white, jagged teeth. Relief washed over me as I melted into the shag carpeting. Now that I had finished my final project, I had time to walk the streets again, searching for another interviewee.

Public works people were scattered along the roadways, decorating streetlights with Christmas ornaments, while vehicles sloshed by through melting snow. As I crossed the long bridge into the heart of downtown, I lowered the brim of my hat, protecting my face from the three-river winds. I thought I'd make it easy on myself and go directly to the mission on the outskirts of town rather than trek all over the concrete jungle, wearing out my joints.

The sun crept through the narrow alleyways, framing sections of storefronts with lambent shapes. It was as though I had stepped through a doorway to heaven. Everything shimmered from the trickling of melting icicles, while pigeons cooed softly from above, creating a soothing ambience.

Maybe it was the otherworldly feeling of the moment, but I felt as if nothing really mattered. Time seemed to stand still as I floated on a cloud of ecstasy. Even the symphonious urban rhythms, pounding from a passing hotrod, seemed to admix with my state of mind.

While the winds brushed the soft snow powder from towering rooftops, the tiny crystals shimmered through soft golden sunrays. I noticed a woman peering at me from across the street. She leaned against a short wall, her backpack propped against her legs. As the glowing red stone on the ring began to pulsate, I crossed the road. A deep knowing enshrouded my mind, as I determined that this woman would be my next interview. The woman's brown skin took on a deep golden color under the light of the late afternoon sun. As I approached her, the gold in her skin faded to a light brown. The pocks highlighting her high cheekbones seemed to create a kind of design, like a "connect-the-dots" page in a child's coloring book. As I hopped onto the curb our eyes connected, followed by a mutual and effortless smile. I guess it was the mood I was in, but as soon as she smiled back I began a dialogue.

"A beautiful day, isn't it?" I said. She just glanced at me cockeyed, as if wondering what planet I was from. We stood there for a couple of minutes watching the cars swash by. Then, as smooth as the gliding tires, I introduced myself, and she did the same.

"Hi, I'm Shercy," she said, keeping her distance, a soft shyness to her voice, like a timid child. I presented my project to Shercy, explaining why I had decided to set out on this journey and briefly recounting some stories from the other people I had interviewed.

As she listened, Shercy became more engaged, as if she related to the stories. As I spoke, her eyes softened, and she became more relaxed. It wasn't long before she agreed to tell her story, as she put it, "for her sisters of the streets."

"I got issues with men," she said, explaining why she had been so standoffish. "But anyway, as long as we stay here, out in the open, I'll share my experience with you. Just for the record, I'm only doin' this 'cause it may help someone else with their situation.

"So anyway, I was living with a man a couple of years ago," Shercy said after taking in a deep breath. "I thought we had something, but it turned out that he was very abusive. He cut me down to the size of an ant. So, one night we got into an argument and he threw me out, just like that. We was both using heavily, you know, crack cocaine and heroin. Anyway, you throw two addicts in the same living space and there's bound to be a war."

My arms began to feel heavy and ache. They felt bruised and raw. The energy seemed to leak from my pores, dripping into the gutter. The city started to spin as I scanned the vicinity and then, to my amazement, I noticed my arms were flowing red with blood. The plasma puddle that surrounded me grew until I was consumed in a deep red pool.

I kept my wits about me, even while Shercy continued her dialogue.

"One night he came home drunk and I was high as a kite. So he just busted loose on me. I not only ended up kicked out of my apartment, but in the hospital with a broken jaw, three fractured ribs, and a bunch of bumps and bruises."

My rational mind struggled as I witnessed my energy body separate from my physical body. It was as though my present state of awareness hitched a ride with my spirit, as I flew high above the lightly sprinkled city crowd. While I drifted off, I witnessed myself down below, still listening intently to Shercy, as if I were an entirely different person.

As soon as I focused on the horizon before me, my body propelled forward, leaving only a cloud of silvery mist. When the cloud that surrounded me dissipated, I found myself in the center of someone's living room, crouched before a coffee table.

"Dear Lord, I'm desperate for your help," a voice begged, from the body I now occupied. "I know I done committed lots of sins. I just need another chance. Please, Lord, give me another chance ..."

The voice of Shercy was interrupted by a loud bang.

"Damn woman!" the intruding voice slammed, "Whasall dis mess?"

A large black man stood towering in the entrance to the living room. The doorway framed him like some horror movie poster. Shercy's vision was blurred. The room seemed perverted and warped, as if she was under the influence of some mind-bending drug.

"I don't want to hear no blaspheme from yer drunk ass, Terell!" Shercy countered.

"Ohhh, is that so, you skanky-ass slut," Terell barked back. "You expect me to just twirl into *my house* and be all sunny, when you've just sat on your ass all day and done nothing? Well, you got another thing comin'!"

Terell stumbled forward, obviously very intoxicated, grabbing for Shercy. She struggled to get away, throwing loose items at her assailant. Terell reached out his large, sweat-drenched arms, grabbing for Shercy. His angry growls turned to mad laughter.

"Oh, come now, baby doll. Daddy ain't gonna hurt ya. I just gonna give you a little switchin'."

Terell's face contorted, like some mad clown.

I shuddered as I witnessed the lunacy unfold around me. Although I was only a spectator to Shercy's past, I winced at the thought of Terell's boulder-like fists slamming into Shercy's moon-shaped face. This was her past, so there was nothing I could do to help—only be a witness and maybe tell her story someday.

The first two blasts were the worst. Before Terell's knuckles made contact, I felt Shercy's hair stand straight, as if there was an electric charge within Terell's rage. The room stretched and blurred. Red pain flares seemed to explode from her eyes.

I wanted to close my eyes and hide from the mania that engulfed Shercy, but I became paralyzed with fear, unable to break the trance I was under. The punches kept coming, and Shercy continued to fight back, landing a few bloody blows of her own. I could not only feel but could hear Shercy's ribs snap, and then the gut wrenching gasps emanating from her depths.

She fought tooth and nail, until her limp body lay outstretched on the blood-stained throw rug. Terell sat spread-eagle on a nearby loveseat. The snakelike smoke swirls from his cigarette streamed through the air as he stared at Shercy. The quiet was killing me, as I lay in limbo within the wounded Shercy. I just wanted to take flight back to my time and end this madness, but I knew I had no control over the experience.

Terell suddenly jolted out of the chair, grabbing all of Shercy's belongings. Shercy shook with fear whenever Terell passed her, not knowing if he would strike her again. He swung the door open, throwing all her clothing into the wet street.

Shercy watched her blouses float through the air, like ghosts on the haunt. Tears rolled down her face, as she realized she was being thrown out into the dead of night, broken and bruised, to fend for herself.

I was shocked to see how gentle Terell was with Shercy as he helped her out to the front porch.

He knelt down and softly spoke into her ear. "Okay, baby doll, you go now, and if you come back, I'll be ready to whoop you again. But next time I won't be so gentle."

The door closed with barely a sound, as Shercy held her side, sobbing in the cold rain. She limped around the yard, retrieving her belongings, stuffing them into a garbage bag.

A cabdriver found Shercy lying in the middle of the road. His shift had just ended, so he drove her to the emergency room. As she lay on the examining table, my spirit peeled away from her, and I hovered inches away from the ceiling.

To my amazement, Shercy stared into my eyes as if she saw me. "Are you my angel?" she asked.

Then I was gone, through the roof and over the treetops, and as I flew, I could hear Shercy's faint voice calling from below.

"I had nowhere else to go but on the streets," she said as I landed smoothly into my body.

"Been here ever since." She said, clearing her throat. "For a woman it's even harder to survive. You got to be extra careful where you go. Womens get raped all the time out here, and if you homeless, the cops don't pay a whole lot of attention to you as if you were well-to-do. Sometimes I dress like a man, see."

Shercy's hair was tucked neatly under a Fedora. She fanned her hand over it, making sure I noticed its masculinity.

"I do this to blend, kinda like camo. You see, this here place is like the jungle—it's male dominated. If I show any signs of weakness my check will be bounced, you feel me?"

It seemed like Shercy was questioning my attentiveness, her eyes squinted, radiating suspicion.

"I know at least two women who got raped and heard about one that gots herself killed. It ain't no joke out here—it's survival of the fittest!"

I became fixed on Shercy's big brown eyes. Vignette-like images seemed to materialize from her retinas. A silent movie of sorts flickered before my eyes. I witnessed Shercy's everyday battles for basic comforts—things like a warm bed and shelter. When she did score a bed, Shercy spent sleepless nights guarding her belongings. She would hold her stuffed trash bag close to her chest, like a mother protecting her offspring from bloodthirsty beasts. And when her luck ran out and the shelters were filled beyond capacity, she would sleep in an abandoned car, wrapping herself with musty old blankets.

My eyes burned from the cold wind, snapping me out of my trance. I felt Shercy's helplessness and saw how she was truly a brave warrior, fighting each day to stay alive. I admired her courage and looked at her as a teacher of sorts.

"The shelters was just kickin' a bunch of people out," Shercy said with sternness in her brow. "Some are supposed to let you stay for three months, but two of 'em was tossin' people to the streets without any notice. The shelters are unreliable sometimes, and depending on where you at, can be just as nasty as the streets.

"One place, that was actually just shut down, was crawlin' with roaches and rats, and that was just the people!" Shercy cracked a smile, followed closely with a light giggle, a seemingly rare moment.

"Seriously, though, I didn't feel right there. Couldn't even take a shower without a couple of eyes followin' my every move."

Images of a dark and dingy bunkhouse invaded my mind, caked with slime, crawling with vermin, and only accessible to the most dire of humans. Just the thought of having to sleep in such a place made my skin crawl. A silent prayer streamed through my mind that I would never have to experience such an ominous situation.

"But there are places that are nicer to stay." Shercy's posture softened. "They're mostly connected to a church—they clean and respectful. I feel safer with them. If I make twenty bills, I'll rent a room at the Eldridge. It beats stayin' out here another cold night."

I handed Shercy a five-dollar bill, even though I couldn't afford such a gift. Having just viewed her story first hand, I felt that the money would go toward a safe and snug room. Shercy gleamed with happiness as she held the money at a distance, as if she didn't expect such a gift from me. I assured her the money was hers, as she stood speechless, staring at Lincoln's blank face.

"This five makes twenty-three bills—that means I can get a room and a bite to eat!"

Shercy's embrace stayed with me the rest of the day. I sat in a café, sipping on hot tea, rewinding my tape recorder and listening to some of the more potent moments in Shercy's story. I felt as if the people I had interviewed were an extension of my family. It was crucial that I share their stories with the world and wake humanity from its slumber.

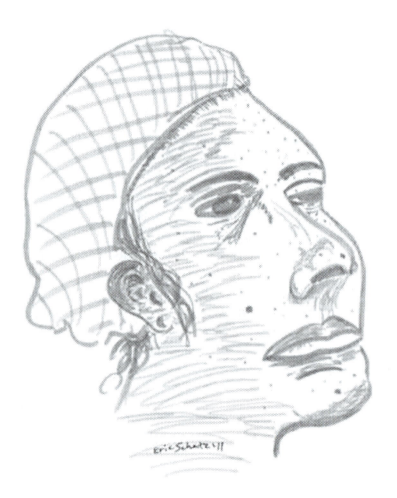

Chapter 12:
Keith

Several of the biggest cities in the U.S., including New York and Miami, say their increased efforts to find apartments and shelter beds have meant fewer people living on the streets or in their cars.

—USAToday.com

Ralph Waldo Emerson wrote, "A chief event of life is the day in which we have encountered a mind that startled us."

My head buzzed from the startling stories and images I had witnessed over the past week. Desperate voices echoed through my mind, bringing me to my knees. I found myself by a riverside, staring at my distorted reflection in the cocoa-brown water.

The laggard current lulled me into a trance as I sat meditating on the slow-floating sticks and leaves that passed by. A great blue heron swooped down from its hidden perch, barely disturbing the glassy water as she touched down. She stood there for a moment before striking her sword-like beak into the dark, murky water that surrounded her.

The catch was a frog. Its legs jiggled as Great Blue swallowed it whole. I pondered how life might be easier for the homeless if only they were more connected to nature: to have all of creation as their hunting ground and to build their dwellings within towering trees instead of in the belly of a filthy dumpster.

It seemed to me that nature ended at the very sight of the city. As I sat teetering on a log, appreciating my place of refuge, I wished there was more green growth and less concrete in this burg. As I began to feel the suffocation of steel, glass, and concrete, I noticed a man squatting before the water a few yards away from me. I could not tell if this man was homeless, or if he, like me, felt adrift on the rough current of this metropolis river. I felt called to approach him. After all, what would it hurt? The sun was sinking behind the towering skyscrapers, so I knew I had another hour to spare before darkness took over.

As I approached him, I noticed he had a fully packed backpack. His clothing appeared clean and he looked well groomed. I knelt down a few feet from him, and he introduced himself right away. It seemed that he was very willing to expose his story to me, as he began to talk before I had a chance to explain my project to him.

I politely interrupted him, asking if I could record his story as I pulled out my tape recorder.

"Hey, I'm an open book. Have at it," he said as he turned to face me. His southern accent told me he was not from here.

"My name is Keith, and I've been out here on the streets for only six days. Now, I say 'only' because there are folks that have endured years on the streets. Six days feels like years because I've been out in the elements day in and day out. I had a good paying job at Welchman's Meat, but I got injured on the job. When I came back, somebody had taken my position and no one else was hiring. I come down to the river for solitude, to get some clarity about my position in life. Seems like the ripples in the water carry my mind to a distant place, a time where things were much easier. Comfort is a rare commodity out here, and when you can get a dose, man, what a treat that is."

The tense expression on Keith's face told me of his struggles and traumas. We focused on the swaying cattails and bobbing mallards that drifted by. He inhaled deeply and shuddered, as if he were fighting off any thoughts of returning to the cold streets of the city.

"Anyway," he said as he wiped his nose with his sleeve cuff, "I went over to the North Side to stay at some relatives' house. But they didn't trust me, 'cause certain family members have been abusing the privilege of staying there. I did feel a bit better knowing that it wasn't just me that couldn't stay there. So here I am, trying to make it through the cracks.

If it weren't for the missions, I would be really down and out. I was on drugs at one time. Crack and booze. I stayed away from the women, because I was afraid of catching AIDS. For one whole year I did nothing but get high and watch as the days floated by."

As I listened to Keith's story, I gazed into the shimmering waters, observing the tiny waves as they slowly transformed into small windows in time. My mind floated into the liquid time machine, and I lingered there, floating amid the darting minnows. As I drifted, I noticed an image of what seemed to be an apartment window.

Keith entered a small room, carrying a bottle of Old Granddad whiskey. He paced the room like a caged tiger. Keith yelled at the bottle he held, blaming it for sentencing him to a life in prison.

I could feel Keith's fear engulf him as he sat on the edge of his bed staring at the door, unable to exit.

"No way, no way can I leave! They'll rip me to shreds out there!" he thought as he rocked back and forth, gripping the stained sheets he sat on. His head collapsed into his lap and he began to sob. The bottle slid out of his fingers. It fell to the ground and rolled across the room, its remaining tonic swashed onto the wood-slat floor.

"Ahh man, that's gonna stain," were the last words Keith uttered before I was whisked away, back to the bank of the river. When I returned, fully in my body, Keith was skipping stones over the glass-like river. The setting sun peeked over the horizon, a sign that my time with Keith was almost over.

"I've had many jobs," Keith said, as he jumped up and down, trying to keep warm. "I've worked at restaurants, a car wash, a doll factory, meatpacking, construction, and janitorial, but there ain't nothin' 'round at the moment. I guess this is my job now—to learn humility."

In that moment, when the sun was slowly fading behind the city skyline, I realized that Keith and I were on a similar path. We were both looking for more humility in our lives. I saw that in order to find humility, we as humans must experience empathy on our own individual paths. The words "Wherever there is a human being, there is kindness" circled my mind. These thoughts were interrupted by shouting down the river. Keith and I turned to see two men arguing over a bottle of wine. Keith and I looked at each other, shaking our heads, knowing what the other was thinking. I felt, in a way, special, as if I had found one of the secrets to happiness. It seemed so simple. Just by opening my heart to another living being, I was able to create a state of euphoria. What a gift!

"I grew up Southern Baptist, so I was always surrounded with talk about 'the Lord' and 'sinners,' but I never really connected to it. It really wasn't until I wound up on the streets, at the end of my ropes, that I turned to a Higher Power. I remember the very moment. I was curled up behind some loading dock, trying to keep warm."

Keith held himself, as if he was reenacting the event.

"As I shook from the heavy cold, without thinkin', I recited the Lord's prayer. Man, I kid you not, as soon as I finished, the warmest feeling came over me. Soon after, I fell into a deep sleep, and when I woke up at the break of dawn, I didn't have no frostbite. It was a miracle!

"When I got saved," Keith said, smiling at the soft hue of the sunset, "I didn't believe that I was saved. Hell, I didn't even believe that I was really a Christian until a day later. On that day, I went up to my apartment, got money, and went out to buy some crack. By the way, this was a couple of months after that one cold night. So, anyway, I bought two rocks, smoked 'em, but felt nothing—the drug had no effect on me! It was like I was in a protective shell, where nothing could harm me. Now, I'm not saying that it was Jesus, or God himself, but it was a divine force.

"So, drugs are gone for me, and now I have to travel alone, without a crutch that is, from now on. There are still tests every day for me, like the other day, when I ran into a woman that I used to buy crack from. She had some paraphernalia in my apartment that she came to get and she also had crack on her. God was definitely testing me, but I passed that test!"

Keith relaxed his shoulders. I could tell he felt more at peace than the past Keith that I had witnessed, pacing back and forth in his cage of an apartment. As the evening closed in, I knew that my conversation with him would end as well. He made his closing statements just as the battery light on my recorder blinked red.

"Now," he continued, "there are people who are drug addicts but have all this money to cover it up with. If they lose a couple thousand dollars, it don't matter, but for those of us living in poverty, it does matter. We're skatin' on thin ice every day, spending our paychecks on our addictions. The only way that the upper class will ever understand poverty is to come down to our level. Now, I don't mean become homeless—I mean to pay a visit to the shelters and missions. They need to open their eyes and hearts to this growing problem. If everyone could play a small part in helping the homeless, we would not have this problem. Even the smallest things like talking to a person about their situation—and like you, writing this book. It may seem small, but it's huge to us folks. People just need some sensitivity and compassion, and need to quit thinkin' about how much they've got or how much more they can get. They need to come out and see for themselves. They will be surprised, I guarantee it.

"Aw, man, look at the time!" Keith said as he glanced at his pocket watch. "Man, I gotta go before someone grabs my bed!"

We thanked each other for the time we spent talking, and Keith rushed off over a grassy knoll and back into the city.

I normally didn't step foot into this part of town in the evening. I felt exposed to the prowling shadows that lurked around me. As fear crept in, I scurried over the same hill Keith climbed and made my way across the busy road, streaming taillights whizzing by, and into the heart of downtown.

I felt shaken by my fearful moment. Was I afraid of some of the very people I had interviewed? Or maybe it was the fear of the unknown. Whatever it was, the streets enveloped me in a deep darkness, a darkness that I needed to face and shed light upon.

As I made my way to my car, I felt deep gratitude for the life I was living and for the warm bed I would return to.

Chapter 13:
Anonymous

While it may be true that a significant proportion of homeless people have mental and physical health issues, problems with alcoholism and substance abuse, none of these are the most common cause of homelessness. The lack of affordable housing was rated third highest (43%) behind mental illness for singles and came out a clear cut winner for families, scoring a staggering 87%.

—homelesstales.com, 2008

When I was a child, Christmas was all about opening gifts and visiting with distant relatives. The thought never occurred to me that there was a family living in a shelter just a few miles from where I filled my belly with duck and pie.

The Christmas after I had begun the interviews was a struggle for me. I was no longer able to see the world with my eyes closed. Instead, I now noticed everyone around me stumbling through their lives, as blind as bats.

It seemed that my whole family was on an entirely different planet than I was. While I sat in the basement listening to old interviews, they went about their normal holiday routine of decorating the tree and preparing the feast. I could feel my grandmother making assumptions about me avoiding her and the group. Because of my paranoia, I would occasionally put my recorder down and emerge from my cave to make conversation.

I spent the better part of the morning trying to take off the ring. I used soap, cooking oil and even WD-40, but to no avail. It clung to me like a parasite, its fangs deeply embedded into my flesh. Or was it me clinging to it? I eventually gave up, figuring it was destiny that brought us together, and it would likely be destiny that would separate us.

As a family tradition, we would all pack into one car and make the journey into town to see the holiday decorations. While most of us "kids" were all grown up, at some point during our time in town we would disband and do some last-minute Christmas shopping, indulging our own inner-children. After finding a suitable gift for my cousin, I decided to take a stroll on the "other side of town."

I had not gotten far before I noticed a man sitting on the steps of a vacant building. Before my family and I left for town, I had grabbed my voice recorder out of habit, just in case the opportunity arose for an interview. What did I have to lose? I had a couple of dollars in pocket and some time to spare, so I rallied up all of my courage and approached the sitting man.

He was a light-skinned, bearded man who wore a heavy winter coat covered by a black trench coat. His eyes glistened as he watched me approach, and as he smiled his whiskers raised, partially covering the tip of his nose. I felt a warmness about this man as he said hello, not even asking for spare change. Our conversation was effortless as we sat together on the crumbling concrete steps.

"Well ain't life grand!" the man said in a joyful tone. "I was just sittin' here thinking that the day is just too boring, and then you come along."

He seemed genuinely happy to take part in the interview as he sat upright and began his account. I had known that we were destined to talk by the way the ring on my finger vibrated and glowed.

"I'm fifty-one years old, on welfare, and I get $204 a month in food stamps."

He chose not to give his name, not because he didn't want to be recognized but because he said it would give him more of a sense of mystery.

"I shared an apartment with a dear friend for fifteen years and this past October he died of AIDS. I could no longer pay rent, so I moved around a lot, staying at this friend's one night and then that friend's the other night. I had my stuff everywhere. In the meantime I had gone back to school at a community college. I was taking up mental-health services. Well, the pressure was too much for me, so I had a nervous breakdown and got sick. So there I am, sick, going from place to place with no home of my own and out of school. My self-esteem hit rock bottom."

He slapped his hands together. A light dust swirled through the late afternoon sunlight, highlighting the right side of his face.

"I lost another friend to AIDS in less than three months later. I guess for me the streets are a place to sort out life," he said as the golden sunrays bathed his head. "I'm not doing too bad at the moment."

His smile looked like a yellow wave of whiskers as his face bathed in the early afternoon sunlight.

"They hooked me up with a counselor at JFK for my depression, and I'm on Prozac. It seems to be helping me, because before I felt like I was sleepwalking through the streets. So now I'm back in school and I love it. It's clean, the ladies are nice, and it's a real good support system when you're not feeling too good about yourself. I come out to the streets from time to time, when I'm low on bread, and panhandle for extra cash. What can I say—it's kind of a habit.

"My solution to the homeless problem is this," he said as he leaned against the cracked brick wall. "There are all these abandoned houses and buildings scattered throughout the city. They should give the homeless jobs to fix up these buildings. This would provide housing for all of us people, and it would give us a sense of worth. We would be creating lives for ourselves. There are places out here that look like Beirut, so they just tear 'em down. They could be used for homes for the homeless."

At this point in the interview, when he was wrapping up, I felt a bit frustrated. I hadn't seen any of this man's past like I had with the other people. I felt like I had lost the gift. It had only been a couple of weeks since my last interview. Maybe I only caught glimpses of people's past traumas, and this man didn't have one to share. Whatever the reason, I decided not to worry about it and just enjoy the remaining time I had with him.

"This is happening in the greatest country in the world. It shouldn't be. There's a breakdown in everything," he said, still smiling, "and the government has money for everything else. On the other side of town they're building a prison. Now, this is a deluxe prison. They have the views of the river and color TVs in every cell. That ain't prison—the streets are. I've become very disappointed in this country. The homeless here are truly forgotten. The prisoners in this country are pampered. The schools in this country are neglected, while money continues to be spent on war. I guess we all need to focus on our own paths, and walk them with pride and happiness. As the good song says, 'God bless the child who's got his own,' and God bless you for doing what you're doing."

He patted me on the back and looked over my shoulder. I turned to look and saw my uncle approaching us. When he got about twenty feet away, I introduced him to the nameless man.

"What man?" my uncle said in bewilderment. I turned to face the man, but he had vanished.

I left my uncle standing, waiting for me, while I searched the alleyway for the mystery man. The only evidence I could find that he even existed, besides his interview on my recorder, was a ripped piece of black fabric from his trench coat that had been snagged on a snakelike strip of barbed wire.

It didn't matter that my uncle would not believe me. I had the man's account taped and would honor his story, just as I had with the others. And for the remainder of the holiday, I enjoyed my family as I had never done before. I truly felt blessed, thanks to the help of the man with no name and his street family.

Chapter 14:
Linda

Freedom is not worth having if it does not include the freedom to make mistakes.

—Mahatma Gandhi

I returned to my apartment on New Year's Eve day. The enormity of the city twisted my gut as I emerged from the highway tunnel. I always wondered how anyone could live among such colossal high-rises. I was here because of school, and when that was finished I planned to retreat to a much greener, more restful place.

I pushed open the front door to my apartment with my shoulder. The weight of the box I was carrying caused me to lose my balance. The box slid out of my hands and its contents spilled all over the floor. I stood looming over the littered floor, thinking about my vacation and dreading my return to school.

As I picked up the mess, I happened upon a newspaper article about the opening of a new shelter on the west side of town. I was more excited at the prospect of another interview than I was about returning to school, where I didn't even feel I belonged.

The morning after my return, I trekked over to the west side, hoping to find another interview at the newly opened shelter. Approaching the location, I noticed a light plume of smoke snaking over a building. As I turned the corner, I realized that the smoke was coming from the new shelter.

Horrified, I darted over to the small crowd that had gathered in the parking lot. I later discovered that someone had set fire to the outer wall, right outside the kitchen. Among the spectators was a heavyset black woman with tightly braided hair. She carried with her a suitcase on wheels, which had bottles and sleeping pads attached to it. I walked over to the woman, plunging my boot in a small pothole filled with slush. She looked over at me, amused by my clumsiness. I limped toward her, shaking the ashy slush from my boot, and introduced myself. She snickered as she presented herself, not sure what to make of me. But as soon as I explained what I was doing at the shelter, she became more engaged.

"My name's Linda. I came down here this morning to try to get a bed only to find out that some jackass tried to burn the place down. They say it's only external damage and that we'll be able to file in later on. It scared me, seeing the smoke and all, because I thought I'd have to be out curb-side another night. Anyways, I'm thirty-one years old, the baby of a family of four. I was thrown out of my house while I was on crack cocaine. I got to flirtin' with this man at a bar one night and he ended up taking me home. He was Jamaican. He wound up physically and mentally abusing me for six months. The fallout of all of that abuse led me to become bipolar—that's a mental disorder in case you're wonderin'. Oh, and I also became manic-depressive. Did you know, statistically speaking, manic-depressives are geniuses and artists?

Now, not that it's glamorous or anything, but I am very talented. I was on crack and my medication at the same time, which messed me up even more. I couldn't do the things I wanted to do.

Being kicked around and mixin' dope wit meds took its toll on me. Man, I couldn't even sit still; I always had to be runnin' around. That was how I coped, constantly moving, 'til I'd end up in some gutter, hair all nappy, clothes shredded and my body throbbin' like that bass beat over there."

She nodded her head in the direction of an old Cadillac. The windows were rolled down, and heavy gut-throbbing beats thundered through the streets. I wasn't expecting any thrill rides with Linda's interview, but I began to feel dizzy and off-balance. I became aware that my reality was about to shift drastically, so I braced myself for the journey. Linda's face warped, like a reflection in some funhouse mirror, and then I took flight.

I pointed my left index finger skyward and began to fly through the now-thin plume of smoke. As I took flight, I listened to the firefighters talking about how nice and smooth this dispatch was. The crowd had dispersed and the sense of urgency seemed to have faded. My body just hovered there, high above the city, and then instantly the world became a blur.

My first thought as I awoke, head between my legs, was, "Be ready for an attack!"

Along with the putrid smell of rotting meat, the room was long, dark and bleak. A buzzing noise from feasting flies could be heard from all around. I slowly raised my head, finding myself face-to-face with a young black woman. As I moved my body, she did the same. It then dawned on me that I was, in fact, the young Linda gazing into a large antique mirror.

Slivers of light cut through thin cracks in the walls of this place. The windows had been blotched out with black paint. I seemed to have landed in a large, musty attic in some dark period of Linda's life. Boxes were stacked to the ceiling, while sheets covered bygone furniture. The putrid stench came from uneaten food strewn across the wooden floor planks.

She wore a thin nightgown, stained with something unknown and ripped down the middle. I could feel her stomach grumble, but she felt numb to her hunger.

"Linda, you eat them scraps yet?" a burly islander voice echoed from behind the seemingly far-off attic door.

A chill raced up her spine and she darted behind a tower of boxes, hiding from the demon man. The splinters in her feet burned as she planted herself in the hiding spot.

I heard mumbling outside and then someone yell, "I's comin' in, woman!"

The creaking of the door sent chills through my body and then a section of the room became bathed in a yellow light. The footfalls seemed heavy, indicating a large man.

"Linda girl, you ain't eat nuttin'. You know I hate it when there's food bein' wasted," the man said as he stood peering through the doorway. "You clean yourself up girl and then you can come out widtherest of da world!" he said before the door slammed shut.

I couldn't understand what was happening in this place. Was Linda being punished for some great misdeed, or was she being held prisoner by this sadistic man?

As I searched for a logical explanation for this mania, Linda crept closer to the fresh tray of food that had been left for her. The nutriment on the plate smelled spoiled, but at this point, Linda could not care less. She needed her life force back, and in that moment she decided to start living.

Linda stared at the now-empty plate. Through her mind flittered images of her past on a seemingly empty canvas. I watched as she struggled through school, dropping out in the tenth grade, became pregnant at sixteen, and got her GED years later. I witnessed her go in and out of abusive relationships and get thrown into countless psychiatric wards.

I saw millions of rainbow-colored pills shower over Linda. She desperately caught the pills and piled them into her mouth. Images of Linda, crouched on a sidewalk as the seasons changed around her, washed by. There were no feelings to these memories—just cold, vacant reflections.

The film flapped to an end as Linda collapsed to the floor. Tears rolled down her face, her body shook as she sobbed and raw emotions flooded out of her once-hollow shell of a body. She began to feel the pain in her limbs and felt her adrenal glands pump fresh energy through her veins. As she got to her feet and realized where she was, Linda began to look for a way out. Scanning her dark quarters, Linda's heart began to race. For once in her life she felt grounded, rooted in a kind of power that had been, until now, foreign to her. As she elevated her body, Linda noticed a skylight, smudged out as well, and in that moment she knew what to do.

Linda's body tingled with energy. Her mind buzzed as she speculated on how to make her exit. The room blurred by while she turned her head from side to side, scanning for any objects that might help her with her escape.

I felt dizzy, consumed with Linda's high-octane animation. It was like riding on the back of a frenzied beast. As soon as she found a small stepladder, Linda swiped a loose board from the floor and headed up the rickety ladder.

The wood slat splintered Linda's callused hands, but she continued without hesitation, like a warrior on a mission. As she stood, teetering on the awkward ladder trying to shimmy open the small skylight, a sound from outside the door made her ears burn. It was the beast-man, stomping up the steps toward the attic. Linda knew she only had seconds to break out of her dark prison. Her hands trembled as the footfalls drew near. After many slippery attempts at jamming the flat end of the board under the lip of the skylight, she finally made contact. Linda pressed with all of her strength as she heard the jangling of keys.

Her hands were moist and slippery with fear, but the window frame began to loosen and then, to her surprise, the skylight shook free. With one last tap from the jagged board, the bubbled window flew open, sliding down the metal roof.

The screeching of plastic on metal alerted the enemy outside the door. I heard his growling and panting and felt as if my heart would explode with anticipation. Linda's feet shifted from side to side as she balanced on the tiny top step of the ladder. The wooden frame jiggled as she reached for the sill above her. Knowing that her worst nightmare was just seconds away from reaching her, she leapt for the opening. I witnessed her dauntless act in slow motion, as if viewing a climactic scene from some adventure saga.

Just then, as Linda's fingertips made contact with the aluminum window-frame, the attic door burst open. As she dangled there, terror on her face, a mighty force surged through Linda's body. Her muscles tightened and she lifted herself without strain through the opening.

Furious, the man below jumped up and down, trying to reach the opening. Fear pulsed through my veins as I saw the rabid beast clawing at the air. Linda watched wide-eyed for a second, taking in her victory, but her bliss ended at the thought of having to get off the roof and to the road.

Linda slid down the damp and slippery metal roof, unable to stop. As she reached the gutter, she vaulted her body toward a nearby cottonwood tree. The cottonwood caught Linda in one of its thick strong branches, knocking the wind out of her. As soon as Linda caught her breath she shimmied her way down the trunk of the tree. She could hear the faint sound of her captor blasting out of the house. She didn't dare look back, and even though her body was twisted and bruised, she kept her eye on the freeway ahead.

The headlights of oncoming traffic trailed by as Linda flapped her arms through the cool night air, hoping to flag down a driver. Just as the bogeyman closed in on her, Linda's prayers were answered. A big rig's airbrakes filled the night, followed by a friendly voice: "Hey there! You need some help?"

Before the truck driver even had time to help Linda in the cab, she was buckled in and yelling, "Go! Just go!"

The driver put the truck in gear and away they flew. Linda melted in her seat. She was finally free and already making plans to disappear from her ugly past.

As I lingered high above the flashing taillights, I scanned the horizon and saw one of the most beautiful sunrises of my life. This was Linda's sunrise, her new beginning, and I felt honored to witness it. As my eyes began to well up with tears, I was yanked away, tumbling back to my time.

When I returned, the firefighters were still planted in their original positions and Linda was speaking in a gentle voice. The lines on her face spoke of her journey, and I now understood where she came from. As she continued to speak, my heart felt heavy for her and what she had gone through those many years ago.

"I changed my name several times, 'cause of him, you know? So, really, what led me to the streets was my whacked-out past and the crack. When I was smokin' the rock, things was real bad. I sold all of my clothes, CDs, and anything else I could get my hands on. I spiraled so far down that I couldn't see no more daylight.

"Sometimes I think that attic prison was better than livin' on these streets, but then simple little things remind me that I am better off now. Things like seeing snow fall from the sky and catching a flake on my tongue. But anyways, I don't much like dwelling on the past. I now would much rather focus on the future, you know, what I want to accomplish."

Linda crossed her arms and held her head high, showing her pride as she sat regally poised.

"I plan to be very successful," she said, as she sat down on the curb. "I'm writing a book about my life and about living with bipolar disorder. I'm just writing this book to spread the message that you can do whatever you want to do. And I want to go to college so that I can help abused people. I used to be a booster, I used to be flim-flammer, a user, and everything in the book. And now I have changed my life. I plan to shepherd the children of the world, to warn them of the dangers that I have encountered."

As I sat next to Linda, voice recorder still rolling, I felt her genuineness and knew in my heart that she could indeed accomplish whatever she set out to do.

"My family is disappointed in me though. They only see what I have done before. They don't see the potential of my future. I plan to open their eyes to the new me. Now, my mind can go into fantasy about what I wanna do, where I wanna go, and who I want to be, but my heart knows who I am and knows my destiny. So I guess I'm just gonna have to follow my heart in order to get off these streets. Like they say, 'Follow your heart and your ass will follow.'"

She slapped her tail end and let out a high-pitched giggle.

"That's all I got to say for now. If you wanna hear more you'll have to buy the book!"

I told her I looked forward to reading her book. Then I gave her a dollar, patted her on the back, and said good-bye. I felt truly amazed at Linda's courage and her commitment to persevere after such trauma and setbacks.

As I watched the firefighters extinguish the last of the embers, I thought of all of the unwanted embers I wanted to snuff out. Linda's story helped me to clarify what direction I wanted to go in my life and I now felt more empowered to move in that direction.

Chapter 15:
Helen

The poverty of our century is unlike that of any other. It is not, as poverty was before, the result of natural scarcity, but of a set of priorities imposed upon the rest of the world by the rich. Consequently, the modern poor are not pitied ... but written off as trash. The twentieth century consumer economy has produced the first culture for which a beggar is a reminder of nothing.

—John Berger

Winter had whizzed by, and spring was now upon me. It was seedtime and the tiny, tightly wrapped sprouts that adorned the low-growing plants began to wake up and unwind. At the same time, my own journey continued within the stuffy classrooms of art school.

It was my final semester and I began to feel the pressure to complete any unfinished projects. I had developed a growing distaste for the academic establishment, feeling like I wanted to throw my projects in the trash and escape on the first bus out of town. However, every time these feelings would arise, my thoughts would drift to my family on the streets and the ordeals that some of them had faced. There were a few that had given up, written off their hopes and dreams as rubbish, and ended up as one of the destitute. Whenever the light within me began to fade, the voices of the people I had interviewed would echo through my mind. "Follow your heart!" they would clamor. "Don't give in to your fears!" they would implore. And I would, time after time, trudge forward, finishing each project, passing each class one by one. Even still, my real passion resided amid the cracked concrete and within the stories of the people that dwelled there.

One day, as I approached the front doors of the school, I noticed a middle-aged woman standing to the side of the entrance. A large duffel bag lay next to her, and she wore clean clothes, yet her shoes were tattered and caked with mud. In a hurry to get to class, I slipped by the woman unnoticed. My focus that day was to turn in all my projects, presenting them as clearly as I could. Because of this, I had completely forgotten about the woman outside. Later, as I exited the building, I was surprised to see her rooted to the same spot.

My ring strobed red. I felt as though this woman was waiting for me, as if she wanted to tell her story. It had begun to rain and the mist from the cool shower waved into the entrance, forcing the woman to press closer to the building. I briefly introduced myself and offered her shelter in the entry area of the building. She seemed neutral about the idea of being interviewed, but agreed after realizing I had just given her refuge from the storm.

"I ended up on the streets because of money problems," she began. "I'm new out here, so I'm just getting used to all of this. The streets are not for the weary. You must be a warrior of sorts to survive. I sometimes don't know who to trust. I think that's my biggest issue. I have been asking for help for the first time in my life. I have learned that if you don't ask for help, you're stuck. I have problems just like anyone else. My problems grew on me until they were just too unbearable. One day, I just couldn't take it anymore. The whole weight of the world seemed to just smother me with fear until I couldn't leave the house."

As I stood listening to Helen's story, rain pounding rhythmic beats against the large windows, I began to feel lightheaded. I felt as though, once again, I was under the influence of some mind-expanding substance. The tiled floor turned iridescent and aquamarine, and whenever I moved, the tiles beneath my feet rippled.

The break room next to us melted into a dimly lit living room. I rubbed my eyes just to make sure I wasn't seeing things, than stepped toward the interior doors. The liquid surrounding my feet felt like

Elmer's glue. It took more energy than expected to move through it. I was captivated by the way my spirit body peeled away from my physical body, like a fruit roll-up snack. My limbs tingled as they separated from my shell and my mind felt somehow lighter and cloudless. The gluey floor now carried me across its translucent waves in the direction of the foreign living room. As I entered the alien room, I looked down at my shoes to see them mutating into someone else's. They were much smaller than mine and Day-Glo in color, but felt unusually comfortable and snug. In the room, I watched as my whole body began a kind of transmuting process.

When I could no longer stand to watch my skin bubble and undulate, I focused on my new surroundings. I noticed a large couch on the opposite side of the room, warm and inviting; there was also a rocking chair, an antique end table, and a blue lava lamp. The room felt warm, unlike the other places I had visited on previous journeys.

My arms began to tingle and ache as though they had been through a vigorous workout. When I looked down at my hands, I was surprised to see that they were very petite and pale, almost ghostly.

God, I don't think I'll ever get used to this! I said to myself as I stood frozen, goose bumps rising and falling all over my new body. I looked behind me and the plate-glass window that used to be there was replaced by an empty bookcase. An antique radiator hissed in the far right corner, soothing to my ears. I began to feel tired, as if I wanted to lie down on the soft couch and fall into a deep sleep. As I approached the seductive sofa, the room began to blur and spin, turning in on itself.

I no longer existed. Helen was in control of my every feeling and emotion. I just floated within her, witnessing her world. She raced around the room, closing, clogging, and covering any opening to the outside world. It seemed that any external noise was a result of some uncovered crack under a door or around a windowsill. She piled towels and clothes against all of the doors, including closet doors, and taped rolled pieces of fabric around windows.

The more Helen panicked, the more the walls seemed, quite literally, to close in on her. All the corners of the room made creaking, spluttering sounds as the walls drew nearer. As I watched the furniture scrape across the floor, I began to question whether what I was seeing had actually happened.

Helen spun wildly, crying out for help, but with all the openings closed off to the outside world, not a soul could hear her. As Helen dove for the couch, I reached my arm out to protect myself from the steaming radiator, forgetting I was in a spirit-body. I felt the burn of the heater as Helen's hand touched it. Her hand throbbed from the deep burn of the radiator as she took cover behind the sofa. I could see images twisting through Helen's mind. The archaic pictures showed figures dressed in black, faces fanged and distorted, hands in a torrent rage trying to claw their way into her home. Helen gripped tightly to the dust-flap of the couch, burying her face in the safety of a cushion.

Hours seemed to float by, as Helen lay still on the floor, her body as quiet as a day-old corpse. I could hear her heart beating slowly, thumping beneath her chest plate. Helen's muscles slowly began to twitch and her eyelids rolled open, and then, like a fiddlehead fern, she unraveled herself and slowly sat upright. A sense of peace filled the dark room as Helen planted her feet on the thick shag carpet. She shook her body and yawned as if shaking off a bad dream, and then, to my surprise, she started to dance around the room.

"They're gone, the demons are gone!" she howled.

But her joyful dance was halted by a threatening sight. A thin sliver of light beamed through an unmasked area of the window. Helen watched as the taped fabric slowly bowed toward the floor, flooding the room with blinding light. The sunlight took the form of golden claws and demonic eyes.

Helen melted to the floor, screaming with agony, "Stop! Please stop! I'll do anything, just have mercy!"

As I departed from Helen's convulsing body, I expected to see the flaming demons devouring her. But instead, I saw her flailing body bathed in a pool of sunlight. She punched, pulled, and kicked like a warrior heroine, while some of the punches were directed at herself, as if the demons controlled her. My heart went out to Helen's possessed mind. I wanted to save her from the flaming claws that made her suffer, but I was helpless to do anything but watch. I turned away from the maddening sight and surrendered to the tractor-beam that pulled me back to my time. As I approached the present, I could hear Helen's faint voice speaking from below.

"Now remember, I had money problems," she said as I slowly came to, "so I was unable to pay rent. Well, one thing led to another, and here I am on the streets, a place I never thought I'd be, facing my fears. I guess if I had to choose my nightmares, I'd choose this one over the past ones."

My hand began to throb and burn. I slipped my glove off and was shocked to find that a rectangular imprint was burned into the palm of my hand. I remembered from the journey that Helen had burned her hand on the radiator and that I had felt the shock of the wound. Had I brought back physical evidence of my visitation to Helen's past?

"I feel like the new kid on the block," Helen said as she took off her raincoat. "I am so naive to the streets. I just know to stick with the people that know the streets, 'cause a person can easily get taken advantage of out here. Now, I haven't had many bad experiences so far. I have only experienced a lot of help. I'm making an effort and I feel that the system is making an effort too. So as long as I continue to move forward, I will continue to grow. And as long as I keep on facing my fears, I will eventually make it home."

Helen reached her hand out to shake mine. I noticed that on her right palm was a rectangular scar, a tattooed reminder of what had happened many years ago. I felt a strong connection to this person, more so than the other interviewees.

The burn had created a bond between me and Helen. And although the scar would fade over time, the memories of her demonic struggles would linger in my mind. As the rain tapered off to a mist, Helen and I stood side by side, watching the headlights rush by. The lull of the sloshing tires made us yawn.

Helen left me with a smile. She seemed to float down the slick sidewalk until the city consumed her. I lingered for a while, revisiting my extraordinary experience, then drifted through the misty streets. Sleep was upon me. I wanted to just curl up in some womb-like cardboard box, but I knew that my warm bed was waiting, calling me home.

Chapter 16:
Anita

Hope is the thing with feathers that perches in the soul and sings the tune without the words and never stops at all.
— Emily Dickinson

I love flowers at dawn, dew dripping from their petals, glistening in the rising sun.

"Is this a dream?" I say to myself as I lay belly to the earth. Feeling warm as I rest in a golden field of wheat florets, free of the stresses of life, my mind is cradled in the love of the earth.

I feel cold shock as I glance down at my clothes. My garments are tattered and smeared with human excrement. The wheat and flowers begin to whither and rot around me and the sky turns black.

"No! Not again! This is not real!" I scream. The ring squeezes the life out of my finger, and the earth swallows me whole. Nothing to hold onto, I melt into complete surrender while the red glow on my finger fades to black.

I awoke beneath sweat-drenched sheets, panting wildly. Relieved it was just a dream, I emerged from my bed to watch the sun rise over the city. I could feel the pulsing of the urban beast as I sat contemplating my next interview.

With graduation looming, I felt an intense sense of relief. Without the restrictions of school, I felt like I could breathe. This gave me the space to focus a bit more on my real passion: delving into the stories of the people I had interviewed. The ring too seemed to release its grip on me, for I could now wear it whenever I wanted to. The ring and I had developed a kind of respect, as though it knew I was committed to the interviews and trusted that I would wear it when needed. So, on this particular Monday afternoon, I decided to slip it on and allow it to guide me to my next destination.

I gave up trying to seek out new interviews. This didn't matter, because I now had the ring to guide me to each destination. The red stone sat on my finger, like a tracking device, stuttering red bleeps as I came upon the right person to interview. I had learned of the ring's tracker abilities when I had been walking for some time, seeking out my next subject, and had begun to feel frustrated, feeling as if my journey was ending. As soon as I surrendered to this feeling, my left index finger began to throb. Lifting my hand, I discovered the blood-red stone beginning to flicker, but only when I pointed it in a certain direction. As soon as I moved the direction of my body, the light would fade and slowly turn dark. North seemed to resurrect the red illumination, so I followed in that direction, until it faded again and then came back when I faced the proper position.

I walked for about a quarter of a mile, arm outstretched as if I were being pulled by some invisible, anxious dog. The soft red glow of the stone mesmerized me, and I became lost in its incandescence. I could no longer feel my body under the ruby's spell. As I stood there on some foreign road, mouth wide open, jaw unhinged with a stream of drool creeping around my lower lip, I heard a faint voice.

"Mister, mister, you okay?" the voice bawled. The unseen person became louder and drew my attention away from the ring. As the spell lifted, I realized that I was standing in front of a heavyset woman, staring down at her Buddha-like belly.

"Man, are you okay? 'Cause you beginning to creep me out!"

I felt embarrassed beyond belief. My apologies seemed to go on for hours as I tried to explain my purpose in being there, but she insisted that as long as I wasn't some serial killer she'd be okay with taking part in my project.

"You know," the woman said as she lit up a slim brown cigarette, "I've been out here for a while now, and aint' nobody ever wanted to hear my story."

She exhaled a plume of thick white smoke, rested her arm on her knee, and watched the smoke spiral through the air. She seemed to be in deep thought, trying to dig up some distant treasure from her mind.

"Well, my name is Anita and I was living in a housing project," she said, breaking the silence. "I started using drugs, and then I got evicted. I was living from place to place, giving the landlords food stamps for rent, and they'd smoke up the money. The project I was livin' in was like a third world country. I mean, there was broken windows and glass everywhere."

Anita extinguished her cigarette in a small pool of stagnant water; the ember hissed as it hit the water. She leaned forward, arms resting on her knees, hands folded in prayer position.

"Man, this shit is heavy. Takes an awful lot for me to go diggin', you feel me?"

I let her know that I was beginning to feel the depth of her story, and then she went on.

"Kids was running around half naked, playing with the glass and chasin' rats. Gangs ran the place—it was the hub of their operation, you following me?" She looked up at me, eyes squinting from the bright afternoon sun.

"So anyways, I had a constant fear of being shot or getting deathly ill. So then I got thrown out and started to sleep in hallways. Man, drugs was everywhere! I mean, you could buy whatever you wanted, especially crack and heroin. At times I felt like I had to be out of my mind on drugs in order to sleep in the conditions I was in, you know, just to vacate for a while."

Anita sat for a while, eyes round as empty saucers, while I stood there feeling awkward, scanning the empty streets and awaiting her next comment. For a moment, the city seemed hushed, as if it were put on pause. Time ground to a halt as soon as the magic ring began to vibrate and my mind began to spin wildly. As my spirit-body took flight, spinning above my petrified physical self, I noticed that the entire city ceased to move. All the vehicles that once skittered about were frozen into place and the people stood still, like tattoos on the skin of the city.

The ring flamed red, trailing my pellucid body around the clouds and through time and space. As I twirled toward the ground, my face tingled from the jet-like speed of the journey. Upon opening my eyes, I noticed that I was sitting at the end of a long gray hallway. At first I thought the place had been hit by a tornado, with all the trash and broken glass strewn about, but then I noticed some movement at the other end, like children jumping up and down.

At this point in my travels, I no longer speculated on where I was or whose body I occupied. Now I merely integrated my energy body into the other person's and surrendered to the situation. I no longer felt fear and trepidation about viewing the person's past traumas. Instead, I would observe their previous life as if watching a movie.

The knee-deep debris made it challenging to move.

"How can anybody live in such squalor?" I thought as Anita's legs plowed through the rubble. It seemed to take over half an hour to move just twenty feet. At times I felt as though I were on some sort of archaeological dig, rummaging through people's personal effects, some dating back to the seventies. I could hear the faint sound of laughter coming from a corridor up ahead. I knew they were children from their high-pitched voices, but I couldn't understand why anyone would let their kids play in such a place. As I turned the corner to peer down the corridor, I saw just what I had expected: two six-year-olds playing in a pile of multi-colored glass.

"What y'all doin'?" Anita's voice bellowed. "You gonna hurt yo-self real quick!"

The two pint-sized ruffians looked at Anita wide-eyed, their dirt-caked faces highlighting the whites of their eyes, making them appear ghostly. As soon as Anita approached them, they skittered beneath an overhang of wreckage. Their bloodied paw prints, cut by the glass, were all that remained, like mysterious petroglyphs on a cave wall.

Inside Anita's head was a barrage of images. She trembled and rocked back and forth as if she was about to collapse from a nervous breakdown. The images became clear of Anita passing out in the middle of the chaos that surrounded her. She lay there, helpless, while wicked predators slithered out from the darkest corners, devouring her very soul.

Most of her fears vanished as soon as Anita sat down on an old, decaying lounge chair. Viewing life through her eyes was like watching a Technicolor psychedelic film. Any movement was followed by a trail of waves and all light would transform into rainbow ribbons. The sounds in this place were not so pleasant as they were amplified ten times their normal volume. The lightest tap sounded like the bellow of an elephant's trunk.

Some of the sensations that arose from Anita were euphoric, while others were most unfavorable. At times it felt as if someone was sticking red-hot needles into her brain, and the pain would bring Anita to her knees. After a few moments of jaw-clenching agony, the pain was gone, and then the visions would start. I wasn't sure if I was watching glimpses of Anita's past, or if the images were some kind of drug-induced flashback from her previous state. Either way, the psychotic slideshow gave me cold chills and made me question my own sanity. The warm red glow of the ring calmed my mind and lulled my nerves, until I was ready to go deeper.

As soon as the smog of my fears cleared, I realized that I was floating through a pulsating dark red tunnel. The tunnel seemed to have built-in film projector screens in the walls. The screens flickered colorful light onto the tunnel walls, exposing its glistening, veiny surface. As soon as my eyes locked onto one of the screens, I stopped moving forward. I was then pulled, as if by a high powered vacuum, toward the flickering images.

My mind seemed to melt into the wavy screen as reflections of a little girl flickered by. She was dressed in a beautiful Easter dress, cloaked with a bonnet and wearing little shiny white shoes.

A voice called out to her. "Anita, come on in now! It's time for lunch!"

Little Anita's beaming, plump cheeks shined like ripe apples in the noon sun as she turned toward the voice. I watched as Anita scampered into her mother's arms. The love that they shared warmed my heart. The great love I felt between Anita and her mother made me wonder how she had ended up on the dark side of life.

The images whizzed by as if someone hit a fast-forward button, then stopped at a different scene. I watched as little Anita and her parents took a family drive through the country. They all laughed and sang joyful songs as they meandered through the countryside. Little Anita peered out of the back-seat window. Her mind was lulled by the fresh glistening rainwater that sprayed off the tires, creating a rainbow effect in the sunlight.

What happened next occurred in slow motion. The tires screamed out, filling the once-serene moment with fear and trembling, and the car spun out of control. The once-joyful drive was now a vertigo hell-ride. Blurred faces of Anita's parents tossed through the air while the car tumbled down an embankment. Everything turned red, just like the roses Anita used to smell when she visited her grandmother's garden. Anita tried to stay with the image of the roses and their velvety petals but was yanked from her moment of comfort by the sound of whining sirens.

Anita's comfortable and loving world had shattered into a thousand pieces. I saw flashes of a double funeral. Anita wore a black dress and watched while her parents were lowered deep into the earth. Everyone around her felt like foreigners, especially the distant relatives who had decided to adopt her.

The arrangement became perverse when Anita's uncle started to act strange. It was as if he had mutated into an entirely different person, a monster. At first her uncle would stand at her doorway while she lay in bed, pretending to be asleep. He hovered there, almost ghost-like, watching her motionless body like some bird-of-prey. Then, as days passed, Anita began to sense a coldness radiating from him.

One morning, Anita awoke to a chilled hand on her thigh. Her uncle held his other hand over her mouth and whispered, "Now don't you say a word, little one, 'cause if you do, the bogeyman'll get ya."

Anita would wake up most mornings fatigued and exhausted, as if she had been drugged the night before. Her stomach would hurt and her inner thighs would ache. She knew her uncle was, in fact, the bogeyman, but was afraid to speak a word of this out of fear that she would be eaten alive by him.

I witnessed a slideshow of painful images of Anita's ordeal with her uncle. Her gums would bleed and sting after she brushed her teeth. It was as if the bogeyman had slipped into her bloodstream, brushed into her teeth, cut into her gums, knocking her out soon after.

I felt helpless as I watched Anita's innocence taken from her. Her uncle's sweaty body would deface Anita night after night, and all I could do was float above them and watch. Out of all of the journeys I had taken, this one was by far the hardest for me to observe. Unable to turn away or cover my eyes at the sight of such a crime brought me to the brink of insanity.

Witnessing the rape and sodomy of any human being is beyond heart wrenching, but when you are inside their body, experiencing every moment of mind-twisting terror, the level of emotional angst is unfathomable. The graphic nature of the unspeakable crimes against Anita's innocent mind, body and soul was earth-moving. Every orifice of my body felt the pain of her ordeal. My skin felt charred and acidic and my head pounded as if a tribal orchestra was playing in my brain.

I wanted to reach out and strangle the life out of the madman who had robbed Anita of so much life, but my job was to be a witness to the origins of her present dilemma. Floating inches away from the ceiling, I watched many heart-wrenching scenes play out and felt deep empathy for Anita's past and present crucibles. I felt that she was a kind of lost warrior who had battled for her life but lost herself along the way.

In a final scene from Anita's past, I saw her slipping out of a tiny bathroom window. She carried with her a small fully-packed knapsack with just enough to get her through a couple of days, until she could reach some kind of safe haven, if such a place even existed. The scene slowly faded to black as Anita disappeared behind a hill. The moon was pregnant that night, illuminating her escape.

My spirit felt limp as I traveled back to my present world. I felt as if I was returning home from a war, heart shredded and soul bruised. When I landed back in my physical body, I was crouched before Anita, sobbing.

"Hey now," she said softly, concern painted in her voice, "you okay?"

I looked down at her tattered, mud-caked shoes and then at my tear soaked hands.

"Oh, um … my God, the things you've been through! What a horrible man your uncle was!" I said.

Anita cocked her head back and tightened her upper brow. "Wh-what the hell? How did you know 'bout my …"

She was mortified and searching for the right words to say.

"My uncle's been dead to me for fifteen or twenty years. How—"

Before she could utter another word, I cut in frantically, revealing everything I had seen from her past. Anita just sat there in awe.

I stopped in mid-sentence, looking up at Anita's bewildered face.

"You think I'm crazy, don't you?" I said, shaking my head at the ground.

Anita leaned over slowly, touching her right hand on my left shoulder.

"Honey, what you just told me rocked my world and brought back emotions I ain't felt in years."

She spoke with sobering tenderness, as if she were a totally different person from the one I had talked to moments ago. She stood up, looked down the dark alleyway across the rubble-filled vacant lots, and was silent for a moment.

"Oh Mama, God Daddy, why'd you have to go?" she said quietly.

Just then, a ray of sunlight cut through the thick gray clouds and bathed Anita's soft, round face. Anita convulsed and heaved buckets of tears as she leaned on my shoulder.

My heart felt tender as Anita released years of pent-up sorrow, my jean jacket absorbing her tears. Without thinking, I put my arm around Anita's broad shoulders. We both stood there, yowling in each other's arms, as the sunlight slowly lit the once-gray alleyway.

As my tears cascaded to the ground, I felt like the stagnant sorrows of my own life exited with them. The ring, which had once glowed with piercing red heat, now gleamed a soft healing purple. It seemed to be telling me, "Now you have truly seen. Now you can truly live."

After a moment of tenderness, Anita wiped her tear-stained cheeks, cleared her throat, and sat down.

"Hey, didn't you want an interview or something?" she said with surprising clarity.

I took in a deep breath and then kneeled next to her, extending my tape recorder, and she spoke into it. Her eyes were wide and clear.

"Man, after that I don't know what more there is to say. Well, okay, here goes," she said with a twinkle in her eye. "Last year, I decided to get some help. This is my first try at sobriety. Days have slid by and nights feel like they never gonna end. So I cashed in all my food stamps and bought some things that I needed—you know, for overnight, basic things. Then I checked myself into a rehab—man, I was ready! Next week I will be coming on eight months clean. This is the first time I've graduated from anything. So now I've got a home group, so I don't go around and get into other people's cases. You know," she said matter-of-factly, "this moment with you kinda feels like a graduation. Like my soul has graduated from my beaten-down past. You ain't tell what's gonna happen next in this life, can you?"

Her question echoed off the dank walls of the alley. I shook my head and acknowledged her with a smile.

"I ain't sleep good last night," she said while stretching her back. I could hear her spine pop like popping corn. "I still have nightmares of hittin' the streets again. You know, I was gonna get my hair done today? I go to Chelsea's salon on Fifth and Eighth. I highly recommend it. She's in the program too. I may have to skip that today—this here seems more important."

Anita's face turned soft, as though she was on the verge of summoning up the innocent child that she had lost decades ago. She continued to speak, this time with a burning passion in her voice.

"A lot of people have become homeless because of drugs. They've got to make that first step to recovery. They got to know that they powerless over that needle. After that, other things will come into play, and their lives will kick it into another gear. I got three kids, you know," she said with pride. "Two daughters and one son! The only one that can come with me is my daughter. She's thirteen. She's now living with my twenty-five-year-old daughter. My twenty-year-old son is with his own family. I go through life feelin' a lot of shame around my kids—you know, leavin' them and all. I feel like I'm a failure as a mother."

Anita's voice softened to a sad whisper. "My kids know that I'm pickin' myself up again and they be rootin' for me. Imagine, after all I put them through, they *still* believe in me!"

Her words sharpened, excitement pouring from her eyes. "The power of love is real! That's what my lesson has been."

Anita and I sat in silence for a moment. It was as if we knew both our lives had changed within that alleyway. As I sat there, with this complete stranger, I felt as if we had known each other for lifetimes.

After all, I had in a sense been through a part of her past, and I now felt as if I was partially responsible for the shift in her life.

"Well," Anita said, "I think this is good-bye, Rick."

I didn't remember giving her my name, but that didn't matter. Two complete strangers had made a heart connection and probably changed each other for the rest of their lives. As Anita and I exited the alley and parted ways, I felt a sense of completion, as if this part of my journey was over. My feet felt rooted to the earth and my mind seemed cloudless. I knew that I could now face life with open arms, and with empathy as my guide, I had nothing to fear.

The fearfulness I had once felt had now turned into love: love for myself, my fellow human beings, and for all of life. As I walked back to my car, I prayed for the preservation of the many precious lessons that I had learned on my fantastical journeys.

Chapter 17:
Passing the Torch

He who has a why to live can bear almost any how.
—Friedrich Nietzsche

I could tell I was dreaming by the way the sunlight cast moony shadows across my bedroom walls. Only this wasn't my bedroom. It was some fantasy place, draped with many different textures of silk and pillows thrown about, like a scene from the *Arabian Nights*. I remember watching the cartoon when I was a child and being awestruck by the harems and their elaborate tents.

I knew I was still in the city. I could hear the bustling traffic outside, but when I looked out the window, a feeling of shock hit me like a garbage truck. All the cars and trucks had mutated into camels and horses, and their riders wore colorful robes. My senses reeled as I inhaled the pungent perfume that floated past my nose.

A man wearing a purple cape stood on the sidewalk staring at me. His smile seemed to call to me. It pulled me down from my room to the walkway next to him. In a blink, I stood face to face with this tanned, gray-bearded man.

He rested his left arm on my right shoulder and said, "Are you ready?"

"Yes," rolled across my lips, and before I could utter another word, our physical bodies had vanished and our particles spiraled in the spring breeze.

I appeared on a park bench, the same one I sat on in a previous dream, but this time I wore a silk robe and was sitting next to a young man whose clothes were in tatters. The dream seemed so familiar to me, just like the dream I had had months ago, but this time it seemed that I was the messenger, while the young man was occupying the space I had sat in previously.

The man sitting next to me shook his head and jolted from side to side. He tried to speak, but his words came out in stutters.

"I-I … wh-what is … this place?" he said.

The young man looked paralyzed. His mouth hung open and he began to shake uncontrollably.

I spoke in a deep yet soft tone that seemed to hush the world around us.

"You will see. You will know," I said without any thought.

"What do you mean, I don't und—"

"You *will* see. You *will* know," I interrupted with a spark in my voice.

The man looked at me with terror in his eyes, and when I looked into a small puddle, I could see why he was stricken with such fright. My body had vanished, leaving only my eyes floating above the wooden slats of the park bench.

The ruby stone floated in my palm as I reached out to the agitated man. The glow of the stone cast a blood-red haze over his eyes. His mouth opened and closed as if to speak, but he was caught in a web of fright.

"Here, take this. It is a gift from the dreamtime," I said as I put the ring on his right index finger.

"Wh-whaat?"

His words seemed to get stuck on his lips, as if they turned to rubber when he tried to speak. Although I floated there, a dream-spirit of sorts, a part of my rational mind remained intact. I thought how amazing it was that I was now passing on the torch to another human being. The ring of empathy had had such a profound influence on my life in such a short period. I felt honored to be a part of its journey. *How many people's lives had it changed?* I thought as I watched the young man gaze into the ring's glowing red stone. I could feel the inquiry building in his mind. Having sat in his seat, I knew what kind of epilepsy his brain was experiencing.

For a moment all was peaceful, until the man tried to take the ring off.

"I-I can't get it off!" he said, expelling terror from his eyes. His body spun out of control, loosening a few of the wooden backrest slats.

"Look at me!" my voice boomed, causing him to halt his fitful panic.

The man's eyes slowly panned in on my floating orbs. We became transfixed on each other, and his dread turned to calm. I had his full attention and I knew I needed to make this moment count.

"Do not resist the power of the ring," I said. "You will follow its glow into the realms of heaven and hell, returning with expanded wisdom. You will understand the *whys* and *hows* of human suffering and develop one of life's greatest gifts: empathy."

The man's eyes turned soft and misty. He relaxed his hand and rubbed the red stone.

"I accept this gift and will be open to the gifts it has to offer me," he said, holding his hand to his heart.

The winds swirled down from above, embracing us, as if to acknowledge the deal between the young man and the ring.

A soft, warm breeze blew through the bedroom window, gathering the sheer curtains, like a spirit-dancer making its grand entrance. My eyes fluttered open, checking to see if the dreamtime had left, or if I was still floating above that phantom park bench. As I rubbed the last bit of sleep from my eyes, my bedroom slowly came into view. Then I knew I had made a safe landing back into my reality. I spent the rest of the morning reviewing my latest dream. I now knew my journey with the ring had ended. I needed to gift the ring to another worthy traveler, but whom?

There were so many people rushing about, not caring the least bit about the homeless problem in this country. How was I supposed to find this person? Finding such a person would be a daunting task. As I lay there on the floor, my head spinning, a sense of calm suddenly came over me. The words "Don't look for him. It is all taken care of" wafted through my mind like the gentle breeze that snaked through the window.

Chapter 18:
Completion

"In three words I can sum up life: It goes on."
—Robert Frost

I could feel the weight of the ring as it dangled around my neck, which is where I now wore it, as it no longer fit my finger. My finger had either grown or the ring had shrunk.

A month had passed since I had received my instructions on finding a new home for the ring. A couple of weeks earlier I had lowered my expectations as far as finding a suitable ring bearer. I knew that if I just let go, the right person would reveal himself.

I felt as if the ring had been my infant child, and now I was searching for the right parent to adopt her. It had been glued to me for the last few months, suckling off my soul, and had become a part of me. I felt torn, not wanting to give it up, but I knew someone else would benefit from its life-changing charm.

The beginnings of fall were all around me, and I felt the heavy presence of death in the cool winds. Change was in the trees, with their leaves slowly floating to the ground, leaving only a skeleton of twisted branches behind. They reminded me of how beautiful death can be, with their vibrant colors that seemed to gleam in the sunlight on every branch.

As I strolled through one of my favorite graveyards, I pondered my own life and the dramatic changes it had seen in the last few months. I loved this cemetery, with its many reflection pools and ponds bursting with golden koi and the polished headstones reflecting in the glasslike waters.

I took a load off on a nearby bench, overlooking a serene pond and a grand mausoleum. My mind felt lulled by the placidness of this place and my body began to melt into the ornate marble bench. All was as calm as the blue skies above, until a distant cell phone rang, breaking the silence and scattering a flock of doves.

My mind whirled into a mad hive of bees. I could not understand why anyone would want to disturb such serenity. I jumped up and searched the hillside for anyone carrying a cell phone, but could find none. As I returned to the bench I had been sitting on, to my surprise, I noticed a man sitting in my seat, talking on his mobile phone.

I was aghast! How could this disturber of the peace steal *my* tranquility? I marched toward the man, my blood pressure rising. I was shocked to see that the man sitting in my beloved spot was in fact the man in my dream!

He appeared to be distraught, as if he were caught in a dilemma. I approached him quietly, careful not to startle him, standing six feet away, waiting for the right moment to speak. His cell phone lay silent beside him.

"Well, aren't you going to say something?" the man whispered.

"Are you talking to me?" I said, my words quivering from my lips.

He raised his head, eyes squinting from the bright afternoon sun. "Who else would I be talking to?"

He sounded annoyed by my question. And even the marble statues that hovered over the reflection pools looked as if they were puzzled, as if they were waiting for an answer from me.

I was stunned. My mind was emptied of any intellect. A feeling of ignorance washed over me, like a timid child on his first day of school. I had been planning this day for several weeks, and now that it had arrived in full color, I just stood there dumbfounded. I felt like a disgrace to the human race.

After standing in silence for what seemed to be an eternity, the man spoke again.

"Well, at least have a seat. Come on over and sit down."

I shook my head to clear the shock from my brain.

"Sorry, man," I said, after taking a deep breath. "It's just been one of those months."

The man rubbed his head and then spoke. "Tell me about it! Hey, do you know anything about dreams?"

His words felt desperate, as if he had been searching for answers for some time. I sat down next to him on the cool marble slab, my mind recapping the dreams that tormented me.

"Well, I've had a few dreams in my time," I said as I gazed into the reflecting pool.

"I just can't shake this recurring dream," he said as he rocked back and forth, cradling his stomach like a newborn child. "It's like it's stuck to me like crazy glue."

I knew exactly what he was going through, but I didn't know what to say to him.

The man turned to me, squinting his eyes and examining my face. "Hey, your eyes—they look so familiar. Have we met before?"

I could tell by the tone of his voice that he was about to remember where we had met. I knew now that I no longer needed to worry about how I was going to explain it to him. The truth was about to reveal itself.

A few moments passed, the man still gazing into my eyes, until I broke the uneasy silence.

"I'm Rick, by the way," I said as I reached my hand out to him.

"Tom. I-I'm Tom," he said dryly.

I drew in a deep breath and relaxed my shoulders.

"Oh my God!" Tom cried, jumping out of his seat. "Y-you ... you're, him!" Tom said, his hand flying to his mouth.

"Him who?" I said calmly.

"The man in my dreams ... the *eyes* in my dreams!"

I softened my gaze and patted the spot next to me. "Please, have a seat. We have a lot to talk about."

I could tell Tom's head was spinning as I explained the mind-bending journey that I had been through. I recounted the dreams that I had had over a year ago, almost identical to his, and then told him of the many life-changing treks into other people's past lives. But I saved the ring for last. I was unable to put its holiness into words; it had to be experienced firsthand.

"This is the ring you saw in your dreams, is it not?" I said, producing the fiery circlet from under my shirt.

Tom's eyes grew to the size of fists. He sat speechless, mesmerized by the shimmer of the blood-red stone.

"Th-that's the one all right," he said with wonderment.

I removed the chain from my neck, unclasped it, and drew the chain through the circle. Then I put the ring on the tip of my finger and slowly handed it to him.

"Here, it's yours now," I said, my mind bewildered by the fact that I was handing this most precious gem to a complete stranger. But I knew he wasn't really a stranger at all, for our souls were connected. I felt a deep knowing that we belonged to the same soul group, or family.

Tom's jaw seemed to unhinge. He sat in suspended animation, just as I had done when I found the precious jewel. He extended his right index finger and then froze in position as if he were under a spell. We sat there speechless for what seemed like hours, until I finally broke the silence.

"Tom, you must put this ring on yourself, for its magical powers can only be summoned by your own freewill."

Tom reached out his left hand and cupped it. I placed the shimmering ring in his palm while he stared at its brilliance.

He gradually grasped the ring with his left index finger and thumb. He slid the silver band around his erect right finger, and the fiery ruby glowed softly. He gazed in awe at the shining red orb, and I knew he had already begun to feel its power. I felt lightheaded; a sense of freedom now flowed through my body. The ring of empathy was now Tom's responsibility. It was his turn to travel into the lives of others and seek to understand their pain.

I felt sympathy for Tom, for he had an amazing and turbulent adventure ahead of him. But I also felt honored to be handing down such a rare gift to someone as worthy as he. I knew that when he was finished, Tom would hand the ring down to another seeker of empathy and the cycle would continue.

As I watched Tom disappear behind a row of sun-bleached gravestones, his right arm extended, following the glowing stone, I pondered my own journey. I thought of all the amazing people I had met and felt deep gratitude for the gift I had been given and the wisdom I now carried with me.

I now knew that the homeless problem in this country, and all over the world, reached far beyond the concrete slab on which the homeless stand. It extended deep within their pasts to places of trauma and often betrayal. It resided in a place of hopelessness, an empty place where the world ceased to exist.

I now know that the only way we can understand the problems of homelessness is to summon our own individual powers of empathy. For the ring of empathy surely exists within each of our hearts, and it is only by opening our hearts that we can access this precious jewel.

Conclusion

Now that you have read this book, I hope you come away with a sense of understanding and, ultimately, empathy. The next time you see a homeless person or someone who is down and out, may you not turn your head in fear or sorrow, but consider the whole picture. May you see past the backpack or shopping cart, and the tarp or cardboard box that they call home, into the pain and dignity of their humanity.

I hope that you will view these individuals not as empty and destitute but as people who have chosen a humble path. For they are here to remind us that we are all one step away from walking in their shoes.